# HAVEN
## by Misty Vixen

D1528295

# CHAPTER ONE

David was now almost positive that he was completely screwed.

If there was a checklist for being screwed in a world ravaged by an apocalypse scenario, then he supposed he'd checked off most of them.

Being alone? Check.

Being under-equipped? Check.

Being in the presence of dangerous, mutant monsters that would gleefully shred his intestines at the first available opportunity? Check.

Being lost? Big goddamned check.

At least he wasn't wounded, but it was almost dark, and it was colder than it had been all year so far. His breath was actually foaming on the air, which hadn't happened until today.

It was a terrible sign that winter was very, very close.

Technically speaking, David wasn't sure he was lost per se, because he wasn't really sure where he was going.

This was new territory, and he'd been desperately trying to find some sign of civilization for the past two days.

Presently, he stood in the middle of a clearing, looking at the mostly dead trees surrounding him, beneath a darkening gray sky, straining his ears to hear if anything was around him. That was the problem with these new creatures: they were so *effective* at murder.

He never thought he'd miss the days where the only things he had to deal with were zombies and assholes looking to rob him.

Those were practically golden days compared to this.

"Shit," he whispered as he turned around.

Something *definitely* shifted among the trees and scrub bushes from back the way he'd come.

He had a vague notion of heading east, but that hadn't gotten him anywhere but woods and more woods so far.

David tightened his grip on the pistol. It was all he had left at this point. He'd had to trade his hunting rifle not too long ago to join the caravan heading for safety and shelter, and now they and it were gone.

Whatever the thing was, it was creeping closer.

He took aim, waiting, heart hammering in his chest, blood starting to pound in his ears. He could do this. He'd done it before.

How many times had he fought for his life? Shot something? Shot some*one*?

Too many to count at this point.

But growing up in a world that had already been devastated for a few decades before you were even born, well...that tended to be an average life for someone who was still alive at the age of twenty four.

What *was* it?

He was in the woods, so it was probably a damned stalker. Those things were horrifying. He caught a flicker of movement between two of the trees and cursed softly again, adjusting his aim. The sunlight was fading, already heading into twilight.

He shifted anxiously. Something moved once more, and then silence.

The tension was really starting to get to him. There was definitely something there. What if it was a person? He honestly couldn't tell if it was getting closer or farther away. Maybe it was a person, and they'd been hiding, and now they were subtly trying to retreat because they didn't know if *he* was a monster–

A maddened blur of movement abruptly burst out of hiding, into the clearing, and started coming right for him.

David shouted and opened fire, but he saw a second muzzle flare and heard another gunshot just barely before his own.

His shot went wild, but the second (or, he supposed, first), shot hit the back of the creature's head and sent it sprawling to the dirt like a ragdoll.

He exhaled sharply as it skidded across the ground and came to rest almost at his feet. It had indeed been a stalker, a slim, slender horror cast in green and brown, and gray as well, meant to blend into the environment. It had long, sharp claws, like black talons, that glinted dully in the fading twilight.

"You were *really* lucky I was here."

He looked up sharply, his mind stuttering to catch up to the situation as he abruptly remembered that someone else was there, and that they were armed. He saw movement among the trees not far from where the stalker had come from.

It was a lot more obvious this time. David shifted aim as he waited for whoever it was to come to him.

It could be anyone, with any intention.

Although the voice was *really* sexy.

"Relax, I'm not looking to shoot or rob you," the person said.

A woman emerged from the trees and he tensed up. She was human and *very* attractive, and that made him suspicious.

He'd seen very attractive women used as bait to lure in horny wanderers before. There were usually armed and armored assholes somewhere nearby, ready to jump on you the second you got close enough.

But...no. She didn't fit. Those women were always dressed very scantily, were always unarmed, and way more...demure.

Nothing about this woman seemed demure.

She had on a leather jacket, reinforced cargo pants, and heavy boots. She wore a large backpack and the handle of probably a snub-nosed shotgun peeked over one shoulder. This woman could probably grab it, aim, and fire accurately in a second. An air of extreme competence hovered around her like a presence.

"Thanks," he said, lowering his pistol.

"Not a problem, I like helping people out. And you look like you need help," she replied.

He fought an instinct to respond immediately in the opposite, because there was a culture out there among the wanderers and travelers, and a line like 'you look like you need help' was often an insult, meant to cut deeply.

But she didn't look like she was trying to insult him. On top of that, he *did* need help. Even if there wasn't something trying to kill him in this moment, he was still lost and alone, with a frigid night on rapid approach.

"I do," he admitted.

"Okay. You want to come stay at my campsite?" she offered.

"I would," he replied, then paused. "You're really just offering? What do you want in return?"

"Nothing," the woman answered. "I just like helping people."

He considered it a moment longer. She seemed

pretty genuine. Was this a trap? Was there some angle he just wasn't seeing?

"What's your name?"

"Cait," she replied.

He frowned, then nodded and started walking towards her, stepping over the corpse of the stalker. Whatever she might be up to, David had to concede that going with her was not only his best bet of survival right now, but his only one.

"What's *your* name?" Cait asked as he joined her and they started walking, leaving the clearing, heading into the dead forest.

"David," he replied.

"Okay, David. So...what the hell are you doing all the way out here, by yourself? You're the only person I've come across today and I've been scouting all day," Cait asked.

He sighed. "I was with a group. We've been traveling for a few weeks now, looking for a place to settle for the winter. We'd heard that there was a settlement in this region and that's where we were going. Then we got attacked by some stalkers and most of the group died, I got separated...that was a few days ago. I'm pretty sure everyone else is dead."

"Fuck, that's horrible. I'm sorry," Cait said. "Well, the good news is that I can give you a relatively safe place to stay for the night, and I can point you towards a settlement. I'm not sure if it was the one you were looking for, but it is a village, and it's not too far away from here. Maybe three hours' or so walk. Most of which is on a road."

"Wow...thank you. Uh, what are you doing out here?" he asked.

"Exploring, adventuring. It's what I do. This was one of my farther excursions. I felt like coming out far this way for some reason today. Good thing for you I did. Normally I hang around the area the settlement is built in. There's a lot around, actually. Some abandoned buildings, some outposts set up, a mountain, a lot of forests, a lake, a river, an island. It's a cool region, actually."

"Huh. So you...live in the village, or..."

"No, not really. Sometimes I'll hit up the inn and stay there for a few nights if I'm feeling lonely or I had a really close call or something. But I'm pretty much a wandering nomad. This region is my home. I've been exploring it for about two years now. Generally I just kill monsters, plunder old buildings, and help people," Cait explained.

"That sounds...interesting," he said. "And dangerous."

"Oh it is, but I'd admittedly rather do this than settle down. Ah, here we are, home for the night," she said.

Her campsite turned out to be a small cabin tucked away in a small clearing.

By the time they actually hit the front door, the sunlight was almost totally gone from the night, and it was very cold. The wind was picking up, and it had a bitter chill to it.

David eagerly followed her into the cabin and closed the door behind him. He saw there were a few locks on it, and he hit them all. Looking around, he saw the windows had been neatly boarded over. They were all uniform and solid-looking boards, nothing haphazard about it.

Although there was only one main room, (there was also a tiny closet and a very small bathroom), it was surprisingly cozy and well-organized.

"Is this like...your place?" he asked. "It looks

nice."

"Thank you, but it's not. Just one of them. One of the many things I do as I roam is find places like this and fix them up," Cait replied as she moved over to a fireplace. She shrugged out of her pack, crouched down, and began getting a fire going.

He couldn't help but check out her ass.

It was *really* nice, and looked almost showcased with how the pants pulled up tight against it. She was clearly very fit, but there were some nice curves to her. David made himself focus. She'd brought him here to be nice, not to fuck him.

Although *man* would that be fucking awesome.

"Any particular reason?" he asked as he got out of his pack and set it down on the floor next to the single bed in the room.

"It's fun. That's why I got started. I wanted a variety of places I could go. But when the new variants started showing up, I figured it would be more helpful to have secure locations scattered across the world. Both for myself and for unlucky travelers like yourself. I leave a little bit of emergency supplies in each one of them."

The new variants.

Just the mention of them sent a shiver of dread through him.

Although he'd been told that the world used to *not* be a large ruin where half of humanity had been turned into zombies, and half the survivors mutated into a variety of inhumans, he found it hard to imagine. And often counted himself lucky.

He'd been born a couple of decades after the great collapse, so to him, zombies roaming around everywhere was pretty normal.

And then, at some point during this year, the

virus that turned some people into zombies, and some people into inhumans, began morphing.

Rapidly.

Suddenly, the zombies became a lot deadlier, and the inhumans, who were immune to the virus, found that they were now capable of turning into deadly nightmarish monstrosities as well.

Nobody knew why this was happening, nor how, only that it was, and apparently everywhere. Or everywhere he'd heard of at least. While before he'd only had to learn to deal with zombies and thieves, now he had a whole array of horrific beasts to survive.

"Aren't you worried they'll get broken into and stolen?" David asked, trying to get his mind off the subject of the variants.

"Yeah, I'm sure it happens sometimes, but it's not like there's a *huge* cache of supplies here or something. And I guess I'd rather help the occasional asshole if it means also helping a lot of good people," Cait replied.

She got the fire going and stood up. She pulled off a black beanie she was wearing and tossed it onto the mantle above the fireplace, letting her hair down. He saw that she had short red hair, and his attraction to her suddenly spiked.

"What should we do about dinner?" Cait asked as she moved over to the door and checked it out. After she seemed confident it was secure, she began checking the windows.

"I don't have much on me," David replied.

"That's fine. I've got some canned beef and some bacon stored here. We can fry some up in a pan. Why don't you get that started? Everything's in that cabinet over there," she suggested, pointing to a little kitchenette area that took up one corner of the room.

He got to it, pulling open the cabinets and tracking down a few cans of beef and some sliced bacon, stored in a plastic container. He found a battered black skillet and an old spatula, and brought it all over to the fire.

"So, tell me about yourself," Cait said as she finished securing the area, then moved over to join him by the fireplace.

"Not much to tell, honestly. I was born in a little village a long ways northwest. When I was eight the village was destroyed by a fire and my parents were killed. A friend of the family adopted me, and we spent the next decade trying to find a new place to settle, but we never stayed anywhere for more than half a year."

"Oh my God, I'm sorry," Cait said. "Why?"

"Something would always go wrong. Bad luck. Sometimes the area was just too dangerous. Sometimes there'd be some kind of natural disaster. There was an earthquake at one point. And then we moved towards the middle of the country, and there were a lot of tornadoes. And then we moved pretty far to the south, but a terrible storm hit one summer and wiped out almost everything. I was pretty lucky to get out of that one alive. There was a lot of flooding. And sometimes there were just no prospects there. The community was too tight-knit, they weren't interested in helping outsiders," he explained.

"Not surprising," Cait muttered. "So...how'd you end up here?"

"Well, after wandering from settlement to settlement for so long, I kind of got used to it. I don't know if I'd say that I prefer it, but it just became my default setting. So I've just been, you know, wandering around," he replied with a shrug. A few seconds passed. "Wow, that got like...kind of dark really fast. Sorry."

"Why? I'm not," Cait replied. "I mean, okay, that came off wrong. I'm sorry about the shitty parts, definitely. But...I don't care that we just met and the conversation took a dark turn. I enjoy these kinds of conversations."

"Seriously?"

"Yeah."

"Why?"

"They're...real." She paused, frowning and staring into the fire.

David took the opportunity to tend to the meal.

"People value different things," she said finally. "I mean, there's the obvious stuff: food, water, warmth, shelter. But then there's the deeper stuff. People put their time and effort towards other things. Some people like to collect things. Some people like to hunt things. Some people like to help other people. I certainly value helping other people, but one of the things I love experiencing, I love cultivating, are real moments of connection. And that's hard to find, honestly. People are so...guarded. But this conversation feels real," she explained.

"That makes sense, I think," David replied, considering her words.

He kept tending to the meat, making sure it didn't get burned.

He did understand what she was saying, and he did know about the connection that could be made between two people. The older people he'd come across still sometimes had curious ideas about how long it should take to form a friendship, or relationship, or to have sex, but David had never understood that.

In a world where you might get your head blown off or your guts ripped out on any given day...

Why *wouldn't* you try to find pleasure and happiness wherever you could?

And he also knew what she was talking about, how rare it was to find real connections. He'd made fewer of them than he would care to admit, but he knew that relationships were on a spectrum, and he'd gotten at least semi-decent at figuring out where whoever it was he was talking to had landed.

A lot of people were guarded, or were only interested in nothing more than polite and shallow conversation, which he supposed was fair enough.

You couldn't go around spilling your guts to whoever happened to cross your path.

There were some friendships that developed naturally over time, but with the lifestyle he had, one where he now tended to stay at a place no longer than a month, or if it was wintertime, three months or so, that wasn't very feasible.

And there was something about Cait, something he'd noticed right away.

"So...in your mind, does this feel like a genuine, rare connection?" he asked.

"It does," she replied, and smiled at him. "I like you. I like this conversation."

He felt another pulse of desire hit him hard in his lower stomach, but ignored it for the moment. "I like you, too," he replied.

"Good! A lot of people don't," she said.

"Wait, really?"

"Yeah. I'm too independent, too headstrong, and...admittedly a little too rash in my decision-making. It's why I largely travel and work alone. I made peace with the fact that I'm kind of impulsive and like to do dangerous things, but I couldn't make peace with the fact that I might be putting other people in danger. I have no problem risking my life, but I couldn't tolerate risking other people's lives," she replied.

"So you *never* work with anyone? I mean, what if people are willing to also risk their lives on whatever it is you're doing?"

"Oh, don't get me wrong, I work with people. I just meant as a general rule. Sometimes I need help and what I'm doing is too important to fuck up, so I ask for help...I think our dinner might be done," she said.

He returned his attention to the meat and the bacon, cooking in the skillet beside the fire. It did look done. She got up and moved back over to the kitchen, then returned with a plate. He took out the meat and heaped it onto the plate, then set it down for it to cool.

While they waited, the pair each pulled out a canteen of water, then settled in for dinner.

For a little while, neither of them spoke, eating the meat after it had cooled down.

"Thank you for this, really. You saved my life," David said.

"I know," Cait replied, then grinned at him. "And you're welcome."

As she ate the last of her meal, she shifted her foot closer to him, until it was resting against his own foot.

It felt strangely deliberate.

He looked up at her, and she stared back at him with intense blue eyes. He felt a pulse of excitement shoot through him, but felt it hesitate uncertainly. He had to be misinterpreting this. She was a *lot* more attractive than he was, and she had to have like a decade on him. There was no way she'd be interested in him.

"So..." she said slowly.

"...so?" he replied uncertainly.

She laughed. "Um...anything you particularly feel like doing?"

"I mean...maybe?" he replied, more uncertain than ever.

She was still looking at him suggestively, and her tone of voice was even more suggestive, but he still could be misreading this, and he didn't want to offend her or look like an idiot. Or have her laugh at him for the mere idea of her wanting to have sex with him.

"Anything, like, *specific* you want to do tonight? It's just going to be the two of us here, alone together...in this cabin...with the one bed..."

"Okay, are you like leading me somewhere with this?" he asked suddenly, at once both frustrated and unable to stand the mounting curiosity of if she actually wanted to fuck him.

"Duh!" she cried, then laughed. "Sex, David! I want to have sex!"

"With me?" he asked.

She burst out laughing. "Well no shit! There's no one else here! I mean, if you're not interested, please tell me, but if you are, which I think you are, because I've seen your wandering eyes–not that I mind–but if you *are* interested, then speak up! Say so!"

"I'm interested. I really want to fuck you," he replied, the words tumbling out of him.

"Was that so hard?" she asked.

"I mean, kinda, yeah. Why didn't *you* just ask from the start?"

She sighed. "I dunno, people tell me I'm too...pushy. Too forward. And I love having sex, and I meet people. Some of them ask me, but some of them don't. And once it was pointed out to me that some of the guys I was fucking who might not be into it...I might be kind of just pushing into sex. And so I try to let guys, and girls, ask me first."

"Who wouldn't be into you?" he replied.

"Gay dudes, bisexuals who just aren't into ladies right now, inhumans who get turned off by humans, straight chicks?"

"You fuck inhumans?" he asked.

"Yes. I do," she said very matter-of-factly. "Is that going to be a problem?"

"No! No, not at all. I was just...surprised. People don't really admit to that, you know?"

"Oh..." she smirked suddenly. "Have *you* been sticking your cock in some inhuman ladies, you naughty boy?"

"I mean...twice, yeah. I haven't had a lot of opportunity, admittedly," he replied. "Why is it I tentatively question whether or not you've fucked inhumans and you get super defensive, but I admit to it and suddenly I'm a 'naughty boy'?"

"I'm just teasing you, David. Really, it's nice to meet a fellow sexual liberal who admits they want to or have fucked inhumans. So...who'd you fuck?"

"You really want to know?" he asked.

"Yeah! I mean, we're about to have sex, this is arousing conversation. Although wait, hold that thought. I want to wash up first," she replied.

"Okay...you got enough spare water?"

She leaned forward suddenly, felt along the floorboards, and pried up a collection of them, revealing a little space beneath.

In it was a small wooden box, and beneath that was a bucket. She pulled both out. Opening the box, she pulled out two bars of soap and two washcloths. The bucket was full of water.

"Wow," he said.

"Yep. Nice, huh? The heat from the fireplace gets into that little niche and warms the water. Or thaws it, if it's frozen. I try to replace it whenever I can. There's a little stream nearby that makes it easy. Now strip, and wash. I prefer my fuck friends clean before I filthy them up," she said.

"Okay," he replied, and began stripping down.

He felt almost electrified with lust right now. How long had it been since he'd had sex? Six months? Yes...about six or seven months. Way, way too long. And it wasn't like it was exactly packed before that, either.

David's eyes became wholly focused on Cait as she started stripping.

She was easily the most physically attractive woman he had ever hooked up with, which only became more apparent as she lost her clothing. Once her bra, which was little more than a very tight, smaller shirt, came off and freed her pale, good-sized breasts, he felt a new wave of intense desire and almost desperate need wash over and rush through him.

When her panties came off and he saw the pleasant thickness to her very firm hips and thighs, and her beautiful pussy, it only got worse.

"So, come on, spill it. Who and when and why?" she asked as she crouched by the bucket, dunked the soap and cloth in it, and began washing herself.

"Yes, right," he said, and pushed past the roadblock he encountered when it came time to take off his boxers.

Being that he traveled around a lot and at least tried to stick to a decent regimen of working out, David was actually in pretty good shape. He was mostly made of lean muscle and his physique was at least somewhat visible.

And he'd been naked in front of women before. It tended to happen when sex was imminent.

But he still felt that intense twinge of discomfort when revealing his dick. How did Cait peel off her own underwear with such apparent ease? Maybe it just came with age and experience. Or maybe it was just who she was.

Once he was naked, he joined her in washing.

"I lost my virginity to a rep," he said.

"Ooh, *really?* Very nice," she replied.

"Really?"

"Yeah! I mean losing your virginity is...okay, it *can* be nice. But losing it to an inhuman...well, tell me how it was."

"It was good. It was really good. I met her a while ago, at one of the villages we were staying at. I was seventeen. We both were. Unfortunately, the village got attacked the next day and we got split up and I just...never saw her again."

"That's awful! I'm sorry," Cait said.

"Yeah. But the only other time I had sex with an inhuman was the last time I got laid, about six months ago. I was passing through a village, I had some spare ammo on me, so I hired a jag prostitute and we...had a great night."

"Oh, give me a break, 'had a great night', come on, give me more than that," Cait said.

"Well...she had an amazing ass. We fucked in missionary at first...and then we switched to doggystyle, and I finished in her pussy...then she let me fuck her in the ass. It felt amazing. She also had access to her own tub. We fucked in the morning in that tub, and then I didn't get a chance to see her again," he replied.

"Why not? She sounds great."

"I was going to, but then the town got attacked by a pack of zombies and stalkers..."

Cait sighed and nodded. "Yeah, I get that. That's happening way too much nowadays." She shook her head. "But I don't want to get into that. Tonight, I want to have fun, happy sex."

"Speaking of which...um...I don't have any protection. I don't *think* I can reproduce, but I'm also not sure..."

"Oh, it's fine. I don't think I can reproduce either, and this *wonderful* virus that mutated so many of us into monsters also pretty much wiped out STDs, which I used to say was a side effect that was worth it, but not any longer...anyway, point is: I want bareback sex. And don't you dare pull out. Even if I do get pregnant, I wouldn't care too much. I kind of want a kid."

"Oh...wow, okay."

She grinned at him. "Does that turn you on?" she asked. "You thinking about getting me pregnant?"

"I mean...yeah, kinda?" he admitted, laughing nervously.

"Oh, don't give me that, I can see your eyes. More than kinda...well, let's make this romantic. And let's...let's pretend you're trying to get me pregnant."

Fuck, he didn't think he could actually get hornier than he currently was, but, well here it was. He felt an all new pulse of mad sexual energy shoot through him and his erection begin to throb.

He swallowed. "I would like that."

She grinned, looking very sultry suddenly. "I would like that too, David," she said softly. "Finish washing. Hurry now."

He nodded and finished up. She moved back over to the niche and reached down into it, pulling out a pair of towels. She tossed him one and he caught it, then quickly began drying off. He actually couldn't remember ever being this horny before.

God*damn* he wanted her.

He couldn't stop looking at her body. She had so much beautiful, pale skin, with the occasional scar. Cait was clearly in good shape, but she also clearly enjoyed good meals. She had a very nice amount of padding to her body.

She did seem like she'd be really good at hunting, which was still probably the best way to get meals. He looked down at her pussy again. The hair around it was short and red.

He loved redheaded women so fucking much.

"Okay, enough drying," she said, tossing the towel on the floor in front of the fireplace.

He agreed and did the same.

They raced over to the bed. As they practically dove into it, she immediately began kissing him, pressing her luscious, hot lips against his own. He groaned at her touch, at her embrace, wrapping his arms around her and hugging her to him.

He loved the feel of her. She let out her own moan of satisfaction as they locked lips and began to share saliva. As she opened her mouth and stuck her tongue into his mouth, he tasted her, her natural taste, and it was good.

A little sweet, kind of strong.

Her tongue sought his, and soon they were

twining and twisting together, wrapping around each other as they passionately made out. David let go of her and put a hand in between them, then began groping one of her big, firm, pale breasts.

She felt amazing.

Every aspect of her was wondrous and he loved how immediately intimate she was with him. In a way, it felt like they had been lovers before. Her comfort and familiarity with him was welcome. But it also had that gleeful sexual rush of being with a brand new partner.

After a moment, she broke the kiss and looked at him with wild eyes. "Let's sixty-nine. I want to be on top," she said.

"Okay," he replied.

"Thanks!" She kissed him briefly, then shifted around.

David laid flat on his back and she straddled his face, settling her pussy over his mouth, and then lowered herself. He stuck his tongue out, seeking her clit, and shivered with excitement as he felt her breath hot against his throbbing erection. He groaned softly as he felt a comforting warmth envelop his balls. She grasped them in her palm and gently began to massage them.

"Oh, you like that, hmm?"

"Mmm-hmm," he replied, and then she cried out as he found her clit and began to tongue it with slow, sure licks.

"Yes...fuck," she moaned. "*I* like that."

Then he groaned as a fresh wave of pleasure hit him when she began to drag her tongue slowly, languorously across the head of his dick. That sent sparks of ecstasy into him, and he was remembering exactly how long it had been since he'd been pleasured by a woman now that he was being forcefully reminded of just how fucking good it felt.

And that was *way* too long.

David didn't exactly consider himself obsessed with sex, but...fuck, sometimes he thought that it alone made life worth living. He just wished he had better luck with it.

Well, he was getting really goddamned lucky right now, at least.

"Mmm...*fuck!*" he groaned as she took his dick into her mouth and began to bob her head. He heard her muffled laugh as she sucked him off.

She was *good* at it.

Her lips felt amazing. He kept licking her pussy, wanting to pleasure her just as much as she was pleasuring him, and from the sounds she was making and the way she was twitching occasionally, he thought he was doing at least a half-decent job.

After another minute or so, she stopped sucking his dick abruptly. "I need to fuck," she said, "I can't wait any longer."

"Okay," he replied.

Honestly, he was about there himself. As much as he loved head, he wanted to be inside of her vagina, wanted to feel the unfiltered, raw, impossible pleasure of bareback sex. Because from what he remembered, it was just the absolute best.

She got off of him and he got up. Taking his place, she spread her legs, smiling at him. "Make me pregnant, David," she said, and he felt a fresh surge of desire and desperate, almost painful, need pulse through him at that.

He had no fucking clue why that was turning him on so much, but fuck if it wasn't working as a perfect aphrodisiac!

David hastily laid down on top of her, eagerly laying his throbbing cock at the entrance of her bare, hot, wet pussy, and then he slipped it inside of her. She moaned very loudly, spreading her legs wider.

"Oh *yes,* David!" she cried.

"Shh! Not too loud," he whispered as he pushed his way into her.

"Sorry, hard to help it. You've got such a big dick," she moaned.

Wow, she was being nice to him. In a way, it almost made him a little suspicious. Women typically only stoked his ego when they were trying to trick him into something, but he still didn't get any of those feelings from her, and right now, he was *way* too drunk on lust to think straight. Plus, honestly, he'd met women before who just liked being nice.

Fuck. Her pussy.

Her fucking pussy was the best thing in the entire fucking world.

He moaned loudly as he started having sex with her, sliding slowly in and out of her. The pleasure burned into him slowly, and he could feel his dick throbbing in response to the stimulation, to being inside of her fantastically tight pussy.

"Yes..." she moaned, staring up at him, her face twisting in pleasure. "Fuck, you feel so good."

"You feel beyond incredible," he gasped, going faster and harder.

"Make me pregnant," she whispered. "Make me pregnant, David. Make me a mother."

"Oh fuck! You've gotta stop with that shit, I'm gonna pop if you keep it up! Your pussy already feels insane," he managed, and he stopped.

"Don't you fucking *dare* stop fucking my pussy!" she yelled up at him, then reached down, grabbed his ass and forced his cock deeper into her.

"Fuck!" he moaned and found that his will was too weak. He really started pounding her pussy, grunting and groaning as he drove into her, making the bed shake.

"That's it! Yes!"

"Fucking take it!" he yelled at her. "I'm gonna fucking knock you up, Cait!"

"Oh God, David, fill me!" she moaned. "Fill me with your fucking seed! Come on! I want you to make me pregnant!"

He let out an inarticulate sound as he started to orgasm.

He absolutely did not want to, and he absolutely wanted to at the same time. David so desperately wanted the sex to go on longer, but his desire to pump that sweet, perfect pussy of hers full of his seed became overwhelming, and the pleasure alone was just way, way too much for him. In a way, he was genuinely surprised that he'd lasted as long as he had.

The orgasm felt like a thunderclap, like being struck by lightning.

It felt like a goddamned seismic event.

An explosion of pure, uncut rapture began in his core and burst outward.

And then it did so again, and again, as his cock jerked violently inside of her vagina. And it only got *more* powerful as he realized that she was coming along with him. She moaned loudly and he felt her vaginal muscles clenching around his orgasming dick, massaging it, and she was getting even hotter and wetter, her body moving against his as they climaxed together.

It felt like one of the most powerful orgasms of his life.

When it was over, he regretted that it hadn't lasted longer, although he had no idea how long it had lasted. Telling time had been beyond him. He collapsed against her, gasping for breath, resting his head on the pillow beside hers.

"Oh fuck...oh fuck...oh fuck..." he gasped, his whole body aching from all the running and other physical activity he'd done over the past week or so being strained by the intensity of that orgasm. It felt like a goddamned full-body one.

"You gonna make it?" Cait asked.

"Fuck me..." he groaned.

She laughed. "Again? If you insist..."

"No, wait, please," he moaned, then winced as he carefully extracted his insanely sensitive cock from her pussy. "Oh my fuck, that was just...that was some of the best sex I've ever had in my life. I'm sorry I didn't last longer, but you wouldn't stop!"

"I'm satisfied with the experience," she replied as she got up off the bed. "We both orgasmed and it felt really good."

"That it did," he murmured, falling onto his back, staring at the old, time-worn ceiling of the little cabin, which was spinning slightly. "Fuck."

"I need to double-check that we didn't get any unwanted company from my noisy display," she said. "Stay here."

She took a moment to wash her pussy with one of the rags, then she came back over to the bed, reached under it, and pulled out a robe. "That yours?"

"Yeah, I keep it here. I don't want to pull all my goddamned clothes back on just for popping outside for a minute. Don't worry, I'll be right back."

She kissed him, then pulled on her boots, grabbed her pistol, and slipped outside. He sat up, waiting, listening. A moment later, the door opened and she came back inside. "Like I thought, I didn't see anything."

Cait rechecked the door and windows once more, then stripped back down, tended to the fire, and then climbed back into bed with him.

"Also, as to your finishing too early concerns, you know we *can* have sex again, right? And I'm really going to want to. In case you haven't picked up on it, I'm a horny woman."

"I'll need a minute," he replied.

"That's fine," she said, and began kissing him again.

# CHAPTER TWO

David felt the bed shift, and then he felt warm, soft skin against him.

A hand on his shoulder, gently pushing him onto his back.

"Wha..." he managed.

"Shh...you have morning wood," he heard a feminine voice whisper. "I've got morning wetness. So I'm going to take care of you and me at the same time. You just gotta lay there, cutie."

Cait, he realized. It was Cait. She lifted up the blankets and then mounted him. He opened his eyes fully and saw her over him, looking insanely attractive, her short red hair an absolute mess, her big, pale tits hanging down.

"Holy fucking God, you are insanely hot," he whispered.

"Thank you," she replied. "You're pretty hot yourself."

She reached down between them and gripped his cock, and he groaned as she slipped it into herself.

Fuck, she was really wet.

Cait immediately began riding his cock and she moaned loudly as she fucked herself with it, pushing him deep inside of her. His hands sought and found her firm hips, gripping them and putting his own hips to use as he began to thrust up into her.

"Oh *yes!*" she moaned.

"Fuck, Cait, this is so good," he gasped.

"Morning sex is the best sex," she replied, grinning down at him.

As they continued making love, his hands couldn't seem to stay still. He let go of her hips, moved back around to her thick, toned ass, and then up, cupping her big, bouncing breasts. Then he slid them around to her sides, moved them slowly down her torso, settled on her hips again.

Cait felt so smooth and soft and hot to the touch, so wonderful to caress and grope.

"Come on...come on...come for me," she whispered.

He was almost there, but hearing her say that pushed him into the wonderful abyss of orgasm, and then he was coming into her pussy.

She moaned loudly and began fucking his cock harder and faster, and then she was coming along with him. They came together, their bodies writhing and twitching in orgasmic bliss, and then they were finished.

"What time is it?" he murmured as he came back to reality, looking slowly around. There was light, but it wasn't the flickering glow of firelight. It was the weak, pale light of very early morning winter sun.

"Barely morning," she replied. "Go back to sleep, David."

She kissed him, and he kissed her back. "Okay."

And he was asleep again almost immediately.

...

When David woke up again, he felt a lot clearer, and he immediately realized that he was alone.

A wave of anxiety settled over him and he fully opened his eyes and sat up. Looking around, he saw that the fire was still going, only it was low, little more than guttering flames and embers now. Reaching over, he touched Cait's side of the bed and found it cold. So she hadn't just left. Where had she gone? Had something happened?

His eyes fell on a slip of old paper on a small table beside the bed. It was resting beneath a battered silver lighter with a flip-top. Reaching out, he collected both items. There was writing on the paper.

*Hello David,*

*I'm sorry I had to leave before you woke up, but I have responsibilities. Don't think this means I don't like you. I'm positive we'll run into each other again if you choose to stick around the area, and I'll be more than happy to share a meal and a bed with you again. You're a great lover and I actually got along with you really well.*

*If you're looking for a place to stay, there's that village I mentioned. It's called River View and you should be safe there for the winter. Keep walking north until you find an old asphalt road, and then follow it west for about an hour and a half. You'll be able to find the village from there. Good luck, David.*

*-Cait*

He couldn't help but smile, at least a little. He was sad she'd left, but well, she'd already done far more for him than he'd expected, so he was deeply grateful for that. And she'd left him this note, and a little gift.

He flicked open the lighter and lit it. A solid flame grew out of it. Quality lighters were harder to come by nowadays, so that was quite the gift. He wondered what he'd done to make her like him so much.

Well, that was just the way it went sometimes, he supposed. Some people he just got along with really well, and Cait was one of those people. Even if she hadn't had sex with him, he still would have liked her a lot.

Snapping the lighter closed, he roused himself. Sunlight was streaming in through the cracks around the windows and door. If he had to guess, he'd say it was mid-morning. Which meant he needed to get his ass moving.

As he began his morning routine, he found it a little bittersweet. David undoubtedly felt better because he'd slept indoors, in a warm, comfortable place, in the company of a very attractive woman, and he always thought that the morning after would be easier as a result. But it wasn't. It was harder.

And the reason for that, he was discovering, was because he just didn't want to get up. It felt too good to stay where he was in that bed. It was, in some ways, a lot easier to get up when you were sleeping on the ground or were miserably cold, because you were already unhappy and uncomfortable.

Transitioning from one state to the next didn't take much effort. Despite that, as he washed up, dried, dressed, and cooked himself some breakfast, he did find that he was in much better spirits. He was happy, happier than he'd been in a long time. There was still that undercurrent of fear, though, that unease, that disquiet.

Because he knew a new threat now roamed the land.

The mutant inhumans.

They terrified him in a way nothing else in his life had before. Certainly zombies had been scary, but when you grew up with them, they weren't *that* scary. Especially after you learned how to avoid, or if necessary, kill them. They weren't particularly difficult to kill.

Bandits and thieves and murderers were scarier, because they laid in wait sometimes, or stalked you, or lied to you. But he'd gotten very good at picking up on ambush locations, and on when people were trying to lure him somewhere. He wasn't perfect, but he was good enough that he was still alive.

But these things…

They were a million times worse.

They were fast, and strong, and devious in some cases.

Some of them traveled in packs.

And they could hunt. Typically, if one of them got hold of you, you were dead. They'd rip your head off or shred your guts out or just tear you to pieces. He'd seen all that happen more than once over the past nine months. No one knew how or why the virus had suddenly made the jump from humans to inhumans, because it didn't seem possible.

The reason being that inhumans were inhuman *because* of the initial virus. Given that David knew nothing about viruses or diseases, he didn't have any theories, and honestly, he didn't too much care.

Why it had happened wasn't so much important as the fact that it had happened.

And it had utterly changed the landscape of survival. A *lot* more people were dying. And now would be the very first winter since all this had gone down. More and more, David wondered if he was going to make it.

He wanted to, but sometimes he wondered why he wanted to. If he was continuing to survive just because it was what he had always done. What were his goals beyond 'stay alive' and 'enjoy himself sometimes'? Well, he did like helping people. He did it whenever he could manage it. Certainly there had been more opportunities for *that* lately.

As soon as David had finished up his meal, he

put out the fire and replaced everything as best he could, trying to make the cabin as it had been before he and Cait had come here.

This was her place, and she had opened it to him, so he wanted to be as respectful as he could. Once the fire was out, the dishware was washed, and everything had been packed back down into the little hidden niche under the floor, he took the opportunity to make sure he hadn't left anything of his own behind.

Once his backpack was secure and on his back again, his pistol checked out and in its holster, and the new lighter in his pocket, he stepped outside.

It was colder today, he was unhappy to see, but there wasn't much wind, which made it a lot easier to manage, and the sky was largely cloudless. He reached into his pocket and pulled out his compass.

Lining himself up with north, he started walking.

…

David hesitated as he heard something.

He stopped in his tracks and looked around, hunting for any sign of threat, his hand already resting on his pistol.

There, to his right.

Something shifted.

He pulled out his pistol and swiveled in that direction in one smooth motion. As he settled into position, he caught sight of movement. Something let out a low growl, and a twig snapped. He swallowed, taking aim, waiting.

Zombie, had to be a zombie.

Sure enough, a few seconds later, the figure came fully into view. It had once been a man not much older than David himself probably, his skin now deathly pale and ripped and decayed in several places. One eye was nothing more than a bare socket, and his clothes were ripped and worn down.

David shifted aim and fired.

A hole opened up on the zombie's forehead and it dropped like a rock. He waited, and when he didn't hear anything else coming his way, he moved forward. After taking a moment to make sure nothing was laying in wait, he finally holstered his pistol and began patting down the body.

It was ugly work, but he was a scavenger, and a scavenger couldn't afford to be picky. It was rare that zombies had anything on them, but sometimes there was a great find, or at least a little bonus. Unfortunately, this zombie fell into that first category.

What few pockets it had left intact were totally empty.

With a sigh, David rose to his feet and kept walking.

He'd been on the move for maybe a quarter hour now, trying to keep up a good pace. It was difficult because he was more paranoid than ever. Despite how much time he'd invested in staying alive and survival tactics, he knew that one of the best ways to do so was a simple mandate: strength in numbers.

Being alone provided a few of its own strengths, but in general, being in a group, or even with just one other person, was overall a better bet. He hadn't been by himself for what seemed like a long time now.

And he found himself missing Cait dearly.

Not just because she'd slept with him or even because he'd gotten along with her so well or the fact that she was clearly good at survival, but also simply because she was another person. He didn't particularly like being alone.

After another five minutes, David heard a gunshot from somewhere up ahead.

Something let out a shriek and he immediately recognized it as a stalker. They all seemed to make the same awful noise. Another gunshot, and someone shouted, a woman, he thought. David pulled out his pistol and began running. He heard more fighting and within ten seconds he suddenly burst through the dying forest and out onto a road.

The road! He'd found it, apparently.

To his right was an enormous woman fighting off a pack of stalkers.

The lean, ugly, ferocious looking things circled her. David aimed and fired at the farthest one, getting lucky and shooting it right through the back of its head. Everyone turned to look at him, and for a second, the stalkers seemed uncertain.

Then the woman, who had to be seven or seven and a half feet tall, a goliath, he knew, kicked the nearest one hard enough that it was picked up and thrown off the road. She aimed and fired the large pistol she was holding, blowing the brains out of another one.

The stalkers split up, two of them turning and sprinting dead for him.

He felt a surge of panic but tamped down on it, keeping his aim steady.

David squeezed the trigger and put a bullet right through the face of one of the ugly things. The other one jumped for him and he shouted in surprise and barely managed to avoid it. Whipping around, he pumped three shots into its back, then blew out its face with a fourth shot to the back of its head.

Turning back around, he saw the goliath woman

stomping on the head of another one, mashing it into an explosion of bloody paste. She suddenly snapped her gun up and fired as the one she'd kicked began to recover. With that last gunshot, they were all dead.

He and the woman stared at each other.

She was very intimidating, but then again, so were all goliaths.

They were one type of inhuman, their mutation making them grow to be an average of between seven and eight feet tall. He'd known a few goliaths in his time and knew that generally they were as likely to do something dangerous as anyone else. Actually, in his experience, they were less likely to do something devious or shady.

All his relationships with goliaths had been, at worst, neutral.

"Hi," she said.

"Hello," he replied. They both lowered their guns. He holstered his first, and then she did a second later.

"Thank you for helping me. My name is Evelyn. But, uh, I go by Eve, or Evie," she said.

"I'm David," he replied. "And, um, you're welcome."

They both stood there a few seconds longer, staring at each other.

He wasn't sure what to say. He wanted to ask her if she'd be willing to travel with him, but he also didn't know if that was a weird question, given they'd literally just met and he knew nothing about her beyond her name. But when she didn't say anything, he finally pushed himself to say *something*.

"Uh, where are you traveling to?" he asked.

"I've heard there's a village west of here. I'm going to try and bunker down there for the winter," she replied, sounding almost relieved. Was she...shy? He had to admit, it was weird to see a shy goliath, but they must exist. Being seven feet tall didn't necessarily rob you of shyness or anxiety, he supposed.

Well, she'd make a great traveling partner, probably.

"I was heading there myself. I ran into someone last night and she pointed me towards it. It's about one or two hours walk from here. It's called River View. Um, would you be interested in traveling together?" he asked.

"Yes," she said, seeming more relieved than ever, "I really would. If you wouldn't mind traveling with an inhuman."

"Oh no, not at all," he replied, and he at least understood *that* hesitation.

Although few humans would outright attack or even cast out most inhumans, there was a lot of tension there. And though it wasn't completely one-sided, as he'd encountered some uncomfortable situations among some inhumans towards himself, he mostly saw it from his own kind.

And that wasn't even counting the wraiths.

He'd begun kind of making it a specific point to help wraiths out if they wanted it. A lot of people treated the half-undeads like shit, and some of them *would* kill them on sight. Though less now, given that there were less options to be picky with who you traveled with or lived around.

David walked forward until he stood next to Evelyn, studying her as he approached. She was very attractive. Her skin had a healthy pale glow and her chestnut brown hair was pulled into a simple ponytail. She was quite...filled out, much like Cait had been, with pronounced breasts and hips and thighs that looked like they barely fit into the cargo pants she wore.

As he came to stand next to her, he realized just how tall she was, as she towered over him. He'd estimate their height difference at somewhere between a foot and a foot and a half, and although that didn't sound like much if it was being described in conversation, he found the reality of this a little crazy. She seemed a bit like a giant to him, not that it bothered him.

They began walking.

"So, uh, you aren't traveling with anyone?" Evelyn asked.

"No. I was. We ran into...troubles, and I ended up by myself," he replied.

"Oh. I'm sorry."

"What about you? How'd you end up here?"

She sighed. "I was traveling with a group as well. We struck out after the village we were living in was overrun by some of the monsters. A huge pack of zombies and a mix of stalkers and rippers. It was awful. The survivors started heading north. We walked for several weeks. Unfortunately, hardly anyone knew anything about the land, as we were all relative newcomers from other areas.

"Things kept happening. Our leader got really sick, and died in her sleep. Some bandits attacked and we lost a few during that. There were a lot of stalker attacks. Three days ago..." she hesitated and fell silent, and he suddenly predicted what she was going to say.

The night she was almost certainly referring to he remembered had been suddenly and brutally cold. "I woke up freezing, and everyone else was dead. We couldn't find shelter, so we made a fire, and I guess it must have gone out in the night, and everyone else froze to death in their sleep. I just survived because...I don't know," she murmured.

"You were lucky," he said.

"Was I?" She sighed. "Well, I'm still here, I guess. I didn't even know them that well. I didn't like some of them because some of them hated me just because I'm a goliath." She paused. "It really doesn't bother you?"

"No, it doesn't. Like it actually really doesn't. I'm not just pretending or anything. I really don't mind. I've traveled with, befriended, and–" he hesitated, wondering how much was too much, "uh, been close friends with inhumans before."

"Close friends?" she asked.

"Um...yeah. We got, you know, close."

"Hmm."

He thought she'd pursue that, but she didn't. In a way, he almost wished she would. David knew he had an odd sexual appetite.

Even if he in no way believed it was wrong to be sexually attracted to and have sex with inhumans, he knew it was rare, based on how often he'd heard fellow humans admit to it. And to be honest, there wasn't a single inhuman type he wouldn't want to sleep with. And there was a kind of immediate attraction to Evelyn.

She was beautiful, and the fact that she was over a foot taller than him only spiked his arousal, for whatever reason. There was a powerful thrill in imagining her on her back, naked, with her legs spread as he furiously buried his cock inside of her. He *deeply* wanted to fuck her goliath pussy…

But he was letting himself get distracted, and

distracted was bad out here, even with a new ally.

He refocused, and they continued their walk along the lonely road.

...

"Wait, look," Evelyn said.

David stopped. They'd been walking for over an hour now, and it had been a pretty uneventful hour. Well, barring the conversation. He was very glad to find Evelyn easy to talk to. They'd been sharing stories and opinions for almost the entire time, broken up only once by having to deal with a zombie attack.

They had stopped before a dirt road that led off into the forest to the left of the main road. Through the dying trees, he could just see a house.

"You wanna check it out?" he asked.

"Yeah, I think we should. I don't exactly have a lot of resources left, and who knows how much they're going to charge to stay all winter..."

"That's a good point," he agreed.

They set off down the dirt road, moving between thick stands of trees. Evelyn looked around and sighed sadly as they walked. "I hate winter. I hate when everything dies. It's so depressing."

"It's pretty bad," David agreed unhappily. He'd been thinking of the forests as dying, but at this point everything was pretty much dead. It had already snowed once so far, even if it had only been lightly, and he had an idea that the first big snow of winter was on fast approach.

What he called the 'fuck you snow', when the skies dumped just a metric shit ton of snow all over the landscape and made everyone as miserable as possible.

"Is there *any* good part of winter?" Evelyn muttered.

"Well...I guess I can think of one thing," he replied.

"What?"

"That feeling you get when it's cold and bleak and dark outside, but you are inside. You're somewhere warm and safe. I don't know, it's a simple but powerful comfort. Although it's about a million times better if you're with a friend."

"I do know what you mean, that feeling. It's a good one," she murmured. She paused. "Would you..." she sighed suddenly. "I don't really do well for friends, most places I go. You seem nice, and like you aren't, uh, afraid of me. I mean, not to call you cowardly or anything, it's just that a lot of the humans I meet are afraid of me, or trying to hide the fact that they're afraid of me, and you don't seem bothered by me...do you want to be friends?" she asked.

"Yes, I would like that," he replied.

She laughed, it was a very nice sound. "Thank you. I honestly think the worst part of all this is the loneliness. Talking to you over the past hour has put me in the best mood I've been in for...months, honestly."

"I'm glad. You seem really nice. I'd definitely like to hang out together over winter."

She smiled at him. "Me too."

They came at last to the house, which was two stories, run to ruin, and home to a car with no tires and broken out windows. They walked up to the car. "Let's get this open," Evelyn said as she stepped up to the trunk.

"You think we might be able to find a crowbar somewhere around?" David murmured, frowning at it. Trunks often gave him trouble.

"No need," Evelyn replied. She got a grip on the indent in the middle of the trunk, grunted once lightly, and tore it open in a sound of rending metal.

"Holy shit, you are strong," he said.

She laughed softly. "Yeah."

They looked inside. There was an old crate with some barely held together clothes, a bunch of trash, and a rusty toolkit. David opened it up and looked inside. The tools on the top were rusted almost into oblivion, but he pulled off the top shelf and managed to find a pretty secure little box. Prying it open, he found a collection of nuts and bolts and nails inside that were in decent condition.

"Nice find," Evelyn said.

"Definitely," he agreed, pocketing it.

He then searched the rest of the car, but there was nothing in or under the seats, nothing in the glove compartment or on the dashboard. With a sigh, he left it behind, and they headed up to the house. It didn't look to be in great condition.

He glanced at Evelyn.

"I know what you're thinking," she said. "Will it support my weight?"

"Well...how about we give it a shot and if it seems sturdy, you search the ground floor, I'll take the second story?" he suggested.

"That's a good idea." She grinned. "We make a good team."

"Yes, we do," he agreed, and again found himself thinking of spending more...intimate time with her.

Was she interested in him in that way? It was hard to tell, or it always had been for him. But he put it out of his mind for the moment. Right now, that didn't matter, because right now, they were doing something dangerous. And it would be stupid to let himself get distracted. They headed in through the front door slowly.

The floorboards creaked ominously under Evelyn's feet, but, after several seconds, held.

"Well, I guess I'll just have to be careful, but I think I'll be okay," she said.

"All right. I'm going to go search upstairs, yell if anything happens," he replied.

"I will. Same to you."

"All right. Good luck."

"You too."

He moved forward, to where a stairwell was covered in the remains of an old, threadbare carpet, leading up to a darkened second story. Reaching into his pocket, he pulled out the small silver flashlight he carried for just such occasions and was glad that he'd taken the opportunity to solar charge the batteries in the recent past.

The beam was decently powerful as he flicked it on. He listened to Evelyn moving around carefully downstairs as he reached the top. A hallway extended to both sides of him and each way was empty.

David had five doors to choose from.

He went to the first one on his left and pushed it slowly open, revealing an ancient, moss-covered bathroom. It didn't smell nice. With a sigh, he set to work searching all the places something useful might be hidden. As he did, he found himself thinking about some of the tenets older survivors and travelers and wanderers had repeated to him over the years.

One of them he'd taken to when he was younger was the belief that there was a certain skill, almost a divination, in being able to find secret caches or hidden gems. And although that *was* a skill, and certainly had its own uses, he now found himself wondering how many things he'd overlooked because of his overconfidence in his own application of this skill.

Because something he had since learned over the last few years was that, unless there was some kind of time factor, persistence beat intuition.

For a while there, it had almost become a point of honor, of only searching areas that pinged his own internal radar, which he now knew was stupid as hell, because there were tons of places where someone might store things from long ago, some of them obvious, some of them not, and some even seemed obviously like places where people *wouldn't* store something, which sometimes meant they would, because they were counting on that.

So David searched everywhere he could see.

The bathroom was a bust, and so were the next two rooms, both of which were bedrooms.

The fourth door led to a closet that had a box on a shelf. He pulled it down and opened it up, and let out a small, happy sound when he found a pretty decent combat knife in a sheath, a little yellow bottle of lighter fluid, a pair of transistors, and a wrench.

A great find. He pocketed it all, and then went on to search the final room, which led to another bedroom, this one the smallest of all. Despite that, he managed to find a small collection of clothing that still looked to be in decent shape.

He had just finished shoving it all into his backpack when he heard a shout and a very loud crash.

"Evelyn!?" he called, shooting to his feet and throwing his pack back on. He rushed back into the hall, down the stairs, and began hunting around.

"Eve?!"

"I'm here, David!" she called back, coughing.

He followed the sound of her voice and found a huge hole in the floor of the kitchen. Moving cautiously up to the edge, he stared down. Evelyn was picking herself up off the floor of the basement.

"Are you okay?" he asked.

"I'm fine. A few cuts and bruises. It more scared the shit out of me than anything else," she replied, her face red. She looked up at him. "You won't, like, tell anyone about that, will you?"

"No, not if you don't want me to," he replied.

"I don't want you to."

"Then I won't."

"Thank you."

"Can I do anything for you?"

"I guess try to finish searching up there. Carefully, though. I don't want you to fall down here, too," she said.

"Okay, is there anything useful down there?" he asked as he began edging slowly around the hole.

"I'm not sure, I'll start looking."

David made his way to the other side of the kitchen, which was certainly her destination before she'd fallen through.

There were rows of cabinets, an oven, and a refrigerator to search. He made quick work of them, given that almost all of them were empty. But, hidden in shadow at the back of one of the cabinets, he found a stash of unlabeled cans. Not that all that many cans had labels anymore, they were kind of a luxury. The places that actually still had canneries could, at best, scrawl a word on there, or even just a few marks, which lost meaning if you didn't know the local mark system. One might mean corn, two blueberries, three peaches, four kidney beans.

So it was going to be a surprise. He slipped eight of them into his pack and then stood up.

"Hey, Evelyn, I found some cans–shit!" he cried as the floor he was standing on suddenly gave out from beneath him.

Evelyn appeared below him and caught him. He grunted as he landed in her arms, and found himself staring up at her. She looked down at him and as they locked eyes, he felt something like a spark jump between them and when the arousal came it was much more intense because of the shot of adrenaline he'd just received.

He almost kissed her, mainly because she almost looked like she wanted him to.

"Thanks," he managed, catching his breath.

"You're welcome," she replied, grinning at him, continuing to stare at him. A few more seconds passed, and again he felt the urge to kiss her, but he didn't, and she finally put him down.

"Did you, uh, find anything?" he asked, pretending to dust himself off while really readjusting his pants so his erection wasn't so obvious.

"Not yet," she replied. "You said you found some cans?"

"Yeah, eight of them, though I have no idea what's in them."

"Fun. Well, let's search this place and move on. The sooner we get to that village, the better," Evelyn said, looking around the basement.

He nodded in agreement and they set to work.

. . .

Another hour and a half later, the pair of them

were standing before a nailed together sign that read **RIVER VIEW POP. 76**, the numbers being interchangeable cards. It sat at the end of a gravel road that extended off the main road they'd been walking along all this time.

The basement hadn't really yielded a lot, but there'd been a few more tools and some clothes in half-decent condition, so it wasn't a total wash.

They walked down the gravel road, and already David was feeling at least a bit decent about his chances of surviving this first winter after the mutations had begun. The people here seemed like they were going about their daily lives.

It felt good to know that, even in the face of all this shit that had happened, life was still going on roughly how it normally did in lots of places. The first building they passed was a three-story structure that had a sign out front, proclaiming it was a boarding house, or basically a long-term inn.

It had **GOLIATHS WELCOME** scrawled on the sign.

"I guess this is my stop," Evelyn said, coming to a halt.

David hesitated along with her, standing there in the road and the cold, looking at her. He'd been kind of building up to asking her if she wouldn't mind sharing a place with him, but suddenly found that he couldn't make himself ask.

It *was* a big question, but he had an idea that she'd be receptive to it.

But what if she wasn't?

"Will you come in with me? Maybe we can both find rooms," she said when enough silence had passed between them.

"Okay," he replied immediately.

Well, living very close to her, in the same building, would be a close second.

Unfortunately, they went inside and talked to tired-eyed jag woman behind the counter, who said that there was only one room left, it was meant for a goliath, meaning that it was big enough that Evelyn wouldn't have to duck to move around and with furniture big enough for her.

"Last I heard, the guy who runs the inn next door was renting out shacks. If you hurry, you can probably get one for at least a semi-decent price," she said.

"Okay," David replied. He lingered, staring at Evelyn for a bit, who looked back at him.

"Come see me," she said.

"I will. It was good meeting you," he replied.

"You too." She stepped forward suddenly and hugged him. He was surprised, but not unpleasantly so. He hugged her back. It felt good, and right, and it lasted for longer than he thought it would.

After letting go of her, he tried to think of something else to say, but couldn't, so he simply said, 'Bye', and left.

...

"All right, this is it."

A balding, middle-aged man with a gruff voice and demeanor finished leading him to the opposite side of the small village, at the other end of the main road that ran through it. Here, a collection of small, ramshackle structures waited.

It was, indeed, a shack.

It looked pretty crappy.

He unlocked it and went in. David followed him

inside. There wasn't much: a single-wide bed, a big sink and a toilet in one corner, a single cabinet with some counterspace and a wood-burning stove in another, and finally a cobbled-together table and two chairs.

"Toilet work?" he asked.

"Mostly," the man replied.

David sighed softly, looking around. One window, covered in barely translucent material duct-taped up. There were holes in the walls that would have to be dealt with, but honestly, it was certainly doable.

"Okay, I'll take it," he said, shrugging out of his backpack.

"I imagine you're planning on shacking up for the winter, right?"

"That's the plan."

"Well, this ain't exactly what you'd call cheap. You'll have to pay every two weeks, and it'll certainly change. Things are a little desperate right now," the man replied, though he didn't sound particularly unhappy about it.

"Fine, what do you want?"

"What do ya got?"

He spent the next ten minutes haggling, and ultimately parted with all of his half of the cans and tools they'd found in that house, and one magazine of ammo for his pistol. And with that, the man passed him a key and left.

David locked the door behind him, then sat down heavily on the bed, which groaned and creaked beneath his weight.

Well, it wasn't what he'd call good, but with a bit of effort, he could certainly make it his for the winter.

In an odd way, he was almost looking forward to

that.

# CHAPTER THREE

One week passed.

David settled into his new home in River View with surprising ease.

He had the idea that it had a lot to do with Evelyn, as he saw her every single day. She was wonderful to be around. She was fun, and kind, and surprisingly awkward. He didn't know why he kept getting hung up on that, but thought it might literally just be the fact that she was a goliath.

Her size probably implied some kind of strength or certainty in his mind, in the same way that when you were younger, you thought every adult had their shit together.

But she made everything better.

One of the first things you learned when you were on your own was: always be working.

Because survival was difficult, and not promised in any way, shape, or form. Even if he was secure inside River View, (secure being a very tenuous term in every sense of the word), he knew that he had only 'secured' two weeks here. And if people decided they didn't like you in their town, they could, and often would, kick you out.

And they didn't care if it meant death sometimes.

Too often, honestly. And so he was going to have to make himself useful.

Which he did. He and Evelyn hunted for jobs around town, and they found them. There were always things to do, and always jobs people were willing to pawn off on other people for a convenience fee. Mostly they pulled guard duty, since while it was dangerous, generally it was more boring than anything else.

But it was less boring with a friend around, and he could immediately tell that Evelyn and him were friends.

It felt very good to have a friend.

Someone paid them to repair their roof, which David actually knew how to do, and Evelyn boosted him up there and chatted with him while he worked, sticking around to make sure that he didn't fall off.

Someone else paid them to move some rocks out of their backyard.

Another job involved replacing a door.

And it looked like Evelyn was going to start picking up steady work as a guard for the inn next door to where she worked, as the owner agreed to give her free food and drink if she hung around six hours a day and basically remained 'on call', in case something happened that wasn't on her shift, and she would agree to show up and help if she was able.

All in all, it was turning out to be a good situation. And David was getting to know Evelyn, and have fun with her, and develop a real friendship with her.

And that felt good in a way he hadn't experienced for what seemed like a very long time.

...

David opened his eyes.

He laid in his bed, staring at the ceiling, listening intently.

A gunshot had woken him up, he was almost certain. That wasn't really a big deal, he reminded himself as he waited, listening for more. Gunshots happened all the time. Well not *all* the time, but they weren't exactly uncommon. It was probably the night watch putting down a zombie, or maybe some idiot showing off, or a misfire, or–another gunshot sounded.

Then someone shouted.

Then another, and another, and then several more.

At the exact moment he saw a tremendous orange-yellow light flare through his window, he thought he heard glass shattering.

David cursed and sat up, throwing the blankets back.

He was almost certain that was a molotov cocktail. As he scrambled to pull his boots on, (he was so glad he'd been too tired to take off his clothes before bed), he ran through a list of things that might be happening, but couldn't help but focus on the most likely one.

Raid. They were being raided.

By thieves, or mercenaries, or psychopaths who just loved seeing shit burn and people die. There were any number of stupid reasons for something like this to happen, but only one real outcome. The yellow light hadn't really died away, which meant something was on fire. Something big. David finished getting his boots on, then grabbed his pistol.

He patted his pocket lightly, reassured at the weight of the spare magazine there, then hurried over to his door. He threw it open and saw someone rush past.

There were more gunshots now, and people shouting, and running feet.

He had to help defend this village, had to get to Evelyn and see if she was okay–

David cried out as, the second he stepped out,

something smacked painfully into the side of his head. The world tilted madly and he went crashing to the ground. Blossoms of pain erupted across his body as he landed, and he tried to get upright.

"Don't even think about it," someone said, and he felt a boot plant against his back and shove him painfully to his stomach.

"Get the fuck off me!" David screamed, bucking.

Another explosion of pain as the boot suddenly snapped out and connected solidly with the side of his stomach. He gasped, wheezing in pain, as he laid there.

"Sit fucking still!" the voice snapped, and suddenly he felt the cold barrel of a pistol against the back of his head. His body froze up, much as he wanted to do otherwise, and he felt another hand begin to rifle through his pockets. "Just fucking sit still you little shit, give me what you got on you," the voice muttered, breathing heavily.

He heard footsteps, heavy ones, getting closer.

Suddenly, the gun disappeared, as did the prospecting hand, and the voice shouted in surprise. He rolled over and stared up in absolute awe as he saw Evelyn towering over him, holding a skinny man in ragged camouflage fatigues over her head. He was bucking and screaming and firing off his pistol. She turned and *threw* him bodily into the side of a building.

He hit with a godawful snap, hit the ground, and stopped moving altogether.

"Holy shit, Evelyn," he whispered.

"Are you okay, David?" she asked, reaching down and pulling him to his feet.

"Uh...yeah, yeah," he managed.

He hurt, but he felt still roughly intact. Fuck, he

realized as he looked down, feeling something in his grasp, he'd even managed to hold onto his pistol through all that. He looked around. Back the way she'd come, towards the middle of town, two buildings were completely engulfed in flames, and even as he watched, a third caught.

"This is horrible," Evelyn said, following his gaze. "We have to help get those fires out."

"Can we even? It's spreading too fast..." David murmured.

There were several dozen people moving around, shooting it out or fighting hand to hand.

"We have to at least chase these fuckers off, come on!" Evelyn snapped, and she ran off into the fray.

David hesitated for a moment, then went after her. She was right. At first, it was a little difficult to tell the difference between who was who, given their attackers seemed to be pretty ragtag. But he had gotten to know or at least identify several of the villagers over the past week, and he located one of them being attacked by two men and set to work.

Raising his pistol, he aimed and fired. The gun jolted in his hand and the round took one of the attackers in the shoulder. The man screamed and whirled around. He raised his own pistol.

David fired again and put a round in his chest.

The man went down.

As the other one turned around to retaliate, the villager they'd been assaulting cracked him over the back of the head with a pipe wrench. His skull cracked with a very ugly sound. David winced. Fighting for your life was an altogether nasty and often mean state of affairs.

He'd done it before, many times at this point.

Although it became more familiar, it didn't quite get much easier. He saw a man fly through the air and spied Evelyn in the fray.

As he prepared to move forward and keep fighting, a new kind of scream went up.

This was one of sheer terror, one that typically wasn't inspired by a person trying to attack you, but a monster. And he watched in horror as, through an opening in the wall midway down the road, near the exact center of town where it looked like the bandits had largely entered through, a stream of zombies was pouring in.

And they were backed up by over a dozen stalkers.

David felt a wave of panic surge over his body, threatening to consume him. He looked around, at the dead and the dying. At the burning buildings, which now numbered five. At the rising tide of undead streaming into the area.

And he made a snap decision.

"*Evelyn!*" he screamed at the top of his lungs. "*Evie!*"

She twisted around to face him, a look of panic on her face, whether from the same reason he was panicking or because maybe she thought he was hurt, he didn't know, but they locked eyes. He motioned frantically for her to join him, to come his way.

She didn't hesitate. She began running towards him.

As she reached him, David tossed a very quick glance at his shack, deciding in a split second that he didn't have time to go in and grab anything.

They had to leave *right fucking now*.

This village was going down and there was nothing they could do about it. If they stuck around, they would go down with it. And so they ran, barreling down the road, away from the knot of burning, bloody chaos. Evelyn bounded easily over the perimeter wall, and David had to stop and haul himself up and over it. He landed with a grunt.

"Where?" Evelyn asked, looking around into the dark, frozen night that surrounded them.

"Away," David replied, and took off.

She joined him.

...

They wandered for what felt like ages through the dark forest.

It was a haunting, harrowing experience, but he stuck close to Evelyn, and she stuck close to him. The only two thoughts going through his mind were: *I need to get away from the danger* and *I need to stay close to Evelyn.* Eventually, a third one started to come down on him as the cold air began to seep into his bones, and it was *I need to get to shelter.*

Finally, he slowed to a stop, and so did she.

"Where are we?" he muttered, waiting, listening.

"I think I know roughly where we are," Evelyn replied.

There were still distant gunshots, but otherwise he'd completely lost track of where the village was. He thought, vaguely, that it was behind them, but that could be totally untrue. He felt insanely, dangerously disoriented right now.

"Where?" he asked.

"Remember when we were out exploring three days ago, and we found that abandoned cabin?" she asked.

"Oh, yeah...we were going to come back and

search it..."

"I think we might be near there."

"Shit, I hope so. We need somewhere to make camp for the night..." Even as he said this, something very light and extremely cold touched his cheek. He looked up, and realized at once that it had begun to snow.

"Fuck," Evelyn whispered.

"Come on," he said, and set off.

They continued walking, this time moving more meaningfully. Minutes went by, and the snow began to come down harder. The wind blew more fiercely. The temperature plummeted. David began to lose hope. If they couldn't find somewhere to stay, they were going to freeze to death out here.

This was a really damned fucked situation to be in.

Right as he felt real panic begin to set in, he saw it.

"There!" he cried, pointing at the dark shape that appeared out of the snowy gloom.

Regardless of whether or not it was the building they were looking for, it was *a* building. It would do. Hopefully. Ideally no one was in it. The pair of them made the final walk through the snow, which was a full on storm by now, and walked up to the structure. They moved along the exterior until David found a door.

He tried the knob, found it unlocked, and pushed the door open.

"Fuck, I can't see anything," he muttered, then began patting down his pockets.

His hand touched on the flip-top lighter Cait had given him and he pulled it out, then lit it. Making way for Evelyn, who had to duck to get into the cabin, he raised the lighter and looked around. Although it didn't provide much help, the flickering firelight was enough to show that the place was pretty abandoned, and in sorry shape.

Most of the windows were broken, what furniture was left was damaged, and there was a lot of trash around.

But at least it counted as inside.

And there was a fireplace.

David walked over to one of two doors that could lead elsewhere in the cabin, ignoring the back door, and opened it up. This one led to a bathroom. He closed it and checked the second door, expecting to find a closet. Instead, he found some stairs.

"Hey, Evelyn, there's a basement."

"That'd be a much better place to sleep," she said.

He moved down the stairs, glad to find them made of solid concrete instead of wood. They descended down to a landing, then turned left. He followed them to the bottom, and looked around at what they had to work with. What he found was more than he expected, more than he'd hoped for, really.

The basement looked a little more habitable, and there was evidence that someone had, at one point over the last month maybe, been staying here. He wondered, suddenly, if this was one of Cait's hideouts.

He studied the room as he made his way deeper in, spying several tables, a couple stacks of boxes, some chairs, an ancient washer and dryer, and...a fireplace! With a nest of blankets and pillows gathered in front of it.

"Nice," he murmured softly, then he spied a candle resting on the mantle of the fireplace and lit it.

He then set about getting a fire ready, glad to see that there was some firewood down there. It was very cold in the basement, he could see his breath. He heard Evelyn shifting around behind him, and by the time he'd gotten the fire going, turned around to see that she was sitting on the pile of blankets.

She looked...shocked.

"Are you okay? You aren't hurt, are you?" he asked.

"No...I'm okay," she replied quietly. "Are you?" she asked, looking at him, seeming to come back to reality a little bit.

"Just some cuts and scrapes from getting knocked on my ass," David replied, then reached up and touched his head gingerly.

"Let me see, I managed to grab my field medical kit," Evelyn said, pulling a box from one of her big pockets.

"Okay," he replied, and located a chair, dragged it over, and sat down in front of the fire.

Evelyn spent the next few minutes in silence studying his wounds. He'd gathered some scrapes on his arms and face. He winced as she cleaned them out, then covered them with bandages.

"Thank you," he said, when she was finished.

"You're welcome," she replied softly.

Thoughts had been rushing through his head, but now he felt tired. Very, very tired. Honestly, it was hard to focus.

How long had he been asleep? He didn't think for more than two hours. He'd been shocked right out of a deep sleep cycle, it felt like. Before they did anything else, figure out what came next, David knew he had to sleep.

As he thought this, he looked down at the nest of

blankets and pillows, and suddenly wondered about sleeping arrangements. As he glanced up at Evelyn, he saw that she seemed to be thinking the same thing.

"It won't be weird if we just share this, will it?" she asked, and her tone of voice seemed to indicate that she needed it to not be weird. Well, it wasn't like there were exactly a great deal of alternative options…

"No, it won't," he replied, deciding to just be easy about this. Besides, he wanted to sleep next to her, to share a bed with her.

She smiled, looking relieved. "Okay, good. We should sleep."

"We should," he agreed.

They did a few things to make sure they were really in a safe environment.

She checked the windows while he checked the door, locking it as best he could. Then they checked in any conceivable hiding place among the stacks of stuff, and finally they tended to the fire, which seemed to be going, and being properly ventilated.

It was about as safe as they were going to get.

He took off his boots and almost started to take off his backpack before remembering that he'd left it behind. Instead, he took off his holster and set it aside, then put his pistol nearby, within reach, just in case. Evelyn did the same.

They spent a little bit arranging the blankets as comfortably as they could manage, then settled in beneath the two largest, heaviest ones. For several moments, they laid there in the dim firelight.

Despite being exhausted, David couldn't sleep. He was too worked up, too anxious, too aware of the fact that a beautiful woman was laying right next to him.

Apparently, Evelyn had similar feelings.

"David?" she asked quietly.

"Yes, Evelyn?" he replied.

"Would you..." she hesitated.

He rolled over and looked at her. She was lying on her back, staring at the ceiling, and he thought she was blushing. She slowly looked over at him.

"I want to ask...would you be interested in, um–" she sighed, suddenly frustrated. "Fuck, I'm so bad at this."

"What is it? You can ask me what you want, Evelyn. I'm not going to laugh or get angry or anything. You're my friend," he replied.

She smiled, immediately looking calmer. "Thank you," she said. "I, um...would you make love with me?"

"I...oh, wow," David murmured.

Some part of him had been hoping, *really* hoping, that she would ask him this. But he was surprised, honestly. He didn't think she'd be into him.

"Yes," he replied, almost before he could even think about it, because this felt right. This was what he wanted.

"Really?" she asked, sitting up.

"Yes. I will, Evelyn,"

"Thank you," she whispered. "I really like you, and I've wanted to ask you, but I didn't want to freak you out, but with all that's happened..."

"It's okay. I've actually really wanted to since we first met, but I didn't think you'd be interested. Um, I've never done it with a goliath before. Will it...work?"

"I've done it once with a human guy before, and it seemed to work out fine then, so I think we'll be okay," she replied.

Evelyn reached under the blanket and began taking off her pants.

David considered it, then finally just undid his belt and the front of his jeans, and pulled his dick out. He was already stiff and rock hard at just the idea of having sex with Evelyn.

"Kiss me," she whispered as soon as she got her pants off and laid back down.

He moved up against her and his lips met hers in the flickering firelight.

It seemed to break through the fog of shock that had ensnared him ever since he'd been woken up by that gunshot however long ago. (Had it been an hour? Two? Twenty minutes? He had literally no idea right now.) It was like splashing cold water onto his face, waking him and setting him alight with desire and need.

Not just for sex, but for companionship, for simple contact, basic physical affection and the feeling that came from this level of closeness with another person. And given that this had been building all week long, ever since they had first met, at least from his perspective, it was a little like tossing a match into a cluster of bone-dry kindling.

David kissed Evelyn passionately, and she kissed him back just as passionately. She moaned, taking his hand and placing it on one of her enormous breasts. He groaned, groping it, slipping his tongue into her mouth. Her own darted forward, meeting his, twining with it in desperate need.

David began trying to get her shirt up, and she helped him. He discovered, as she pulled her shirt up over her bare breasts, that she wasn't wearing anything underneath. He began groping her huge, bare tits, squeezing and massaging them in his grasp.

They were *huge*! Enormous, gigantic, wonderfully, erotically titanic breasts.

"Please," she gasped, breaking the kiss, "please make love to me, now. I need you."

He responded by getting in between her tremendously thick, large thighs. She spread her legs wide for him, showing him her pussy. He saw a gathering of dark pubic hair above it and felt a fresh wave of lust snap through him. He had to be inside of her. David quickly got up against her, overwhelmed by intensely desperate need, and laid his cock at the entrance of her pussy.

Evelyn shivered at the physical contact.

He pushed his way inside of her.

It felt amazing. Any anxieties he had about their size difference disappeared as he pushed his cock into her yielding pussy, and felt the pleasure that came from unprotected sex. She wasn't as tight as Cait had been, but this was definitely working.

And she was *wet*. Goddamn was she so wet! It felt incredible. He moaned loudly as he began thrusting into her.

"Oh my God, David, yes!" she cried, bringing her knees up and spreading her legs out wider.

His head came up to just below her breasts, and he reached up, groping one, staring up at her enormous tits, at her pink nipples.

This was absolutely incredible. He'd fantasized, at one point or another, about having sex with all of the various inhuman women. Even wraiths, the half-undeads. And he'd always wondered if the size difference between humans and goliaths would ever weird him out in some way, if it would interrupt the flow of sex, the enjoyment of it.

He was extremely happy to know that no, this

was not the case at all.

It was a deeply erotic experience.

Fucking a woman over a foot taller than him filled him with intense pleasure and stomach-boiling lust and excitement and satisfaction. Her pussy felt stellar. And, fuck, the way she was moaning, moving against him, begging him for more, moaning his name...this was one of the hottest sexual encounters he'd ever had.

And it really, really helped that he liked her so much.

He'd gotten to know her well over the past week. He liked her, he trusted her, he wanted to be around her. He felt that all important *connection* with Evelyn, and it was made all the more powerful by the fact that it seemed like she felt the same way. She was always seeking him out, carrying on conversations that lasted for hours. He didn't really see her with anyone else, and he certainly hadn't been hanging around anyone else.

"How does it feel, David?" she whispered, panting. "How does my pussy feel? Do you love it?"

"I love it," he moaned. "I love your pussy, Evelyn. I love it so much. It feels amazing."

"Good...fuck, I love your cock," she groaned loudly. "Don't fucking stop," she begged.

He kept going, hammering her pussy, burying his whole length inside of her again and again, really pounding her. She could take it, given her size, and she seemed to want it like that. Her body responded well to the treatment, and he was certainly enjoying it.

David lost himself inside of her, lost track of time. All he knew was that they were making passionate love, and it felt incredible, and it didn't leave room for anything else. At some point though, like all good things, it had to end.

But not before a huge orgasm.

"Can I come in you?" he moaned eventually, when he knew he was close.

"Yes. Keep going, just a little bit longer, I'm so close..." she gasped in reply.

"Okay...okay, Evelyn," he panted.

He kept going, pounding that perfect goliath pussy, and suddenly she triggered. Her whole body twitched, and she let out a loud cry of bliss.

"Oh *David!*" she screamed, and he felt her start to come.

Her pussy got wetter and hotter, and convulsed around his rigid length, squeezing and massaging it, and that instantly rocketed him off into orgasmic oblivion. He cried out as his dick squeezed and then kicked, his whole body going rigid, and his hips jerking automatically in time with his orgasm. He began shooting thick loads of his seed out, pumping her pussy full of it, hosing down her insides with the stuff.

It felt like gallons were coming out of him.

They came together, lost in the tempest sea of mind-blasting pleasure and sexual gratification, and eventually were returned, gradually washing up on the shores of post-orgasmic bliss. And David found himself covered in sweat, laying against her, gasping for breath.

He felt himself rising and falling as she panted for breath as well.

"Oh fuck, that was incredible," she whispered. "David, that was wonderful."

"It was, Evelyn. It was amazing. I loved that," he replied.

"Good," she said, wrapping her arms carefully around him, "I did, too. I was a little scared you wouldn't be into it, if I'm being honest."

"Why?" he asked.

"I know you like me, I can see that, but even people who've liked me before, I mean, even like *liked* me in this way, they often can't get past the size difference. But I feel like it really didn't bother you at all."

"It didn't," he was happy to confirm. "It didn't. I like you so much, Evelyn."

"Okay–" she broke off with a huge yawn. "Oh wow, I'm sorry. I'm just dead tired now."

"Me too," he replied after a big yawn of his own. "We really need sleep."

"Uh-huh. Then we'll figure this out in the morning."

He wondered if she meant this sudden shift in their relationship, or the dire new circumstances they found themselves in. Maybe both.

Well, she was right. In the morning.

He pulled out of her and laid down beside her. They curled up together as best they could, and then he immediately fell asleep.

# CHAPTER FOUR

When David woke up, it was dark, but warm.

He didn't know where he was at first, but that didn't concern him. He had a sense that there had been danger, but it had passed, and he was safe now. Wherever he was, it was safe there. The first knowledge he regained was that he was lying next to Evelyn.

There was dim light coming from somewhere, and in it, he could see that she was lying on her side, facing towards him. She was topless, and he could see her enormous breasts swaying gently as she breathed. She was asleep, and she looked remarkably beautiful.

Other things came to him.

He was indoors.

Bad things had happened last night.

He was hungry, and he had to take a leak.

As he was thinking these things, Evelyn opened her eyes. She smiled when she saw him looking at her. "Hi," she said.

"Hello," he replied.

"You were watching me sleep."

"I guess I was."

"Normally that would kind of freak me out but...I like that you were doing it."

"You look really pretty," he replied.

She smiled wider. "Thank you."

Another few seconds passed, and then Evelyn slowly sat up. She was blushing. "So I guess um, we should talk about last night."

"Which part? Because there's a lot to unpack there, I think," he replied.

She laughed. "Yeah, there really is. Well, before

anything else, I guess I want to say...thank you, for fucking me. That was really, really good. And, I mean, if it was just like a 'heat-of-the-moment' kind of thing, like, you don't want to do it again, I'll understand."

"I want to do it again," he replied. "I want to do it as often as you're interested."

"Oh wow," she murmured, looking surprised. "I– really? Like, seriously?"

"Yeah. I mean, why the fuck wouldn't I? That really was great. That was incredible sex, and I like you a lot, and I mean, if you're interested, then I'm interested."

"I am *definitely* interested. It's just that...I mean, like I was saying earlier–I mean, sex between the species is always kind of a tricky subject. But there's kind of a second level to sex between a goliath and anyone else. I mean, we're so much bigger than all the other species. Coupling between us and any other species isn't exactly rare, but it *is* less common.

"So you can understand why I'm more prepared to believe that someone from another species isn't interested in me, rather than is. And like real relationships, not just sex, is even rarer." She paused, and blushed more fiercely. "I mean, um-uh, not that I'm necessarily saying that that's what we need to have..."

"Do you want to be a couple?" David asked.

She chewed on her lower lip and looked away. "I mean...yeah," she said quietly. She looked back suddenly. "But I don't want to pressure you into anything."

"Evelyn, this past week has been amazing. I love talking with you, I love having sex with you, I love just spending time with you. I want to be your boyfriend, and I want you to be my girlfriend. I mean, in my mind, we're already going to be spending the winter together, and we'll be relying on each other more than ever given our present situation. I mean, I think that's going to make us a couple anyway, so we might as well acknowledge it."

"I am in full agreement with this," she said, beaming with a huge smile. It was the sun breaking through the clouds on a dark, miserable day.

"I'm glad," he replied, then hesitated as he recalled something. "Although, given this change, there *is* something I should probably address..."

"Is it another girl?" Evelyn asked after a few seconds, smirking.

"Yes. Sort of."

"Tell me about her."

"The night before we met, I was rescued by a local. A human named Cait. She came onto me pretty heavily and we had...well, amazing sex. She said she'd love to be with me again if we ever run into each other. I don't know how likely that is, but I wanted to know how you wanted to handle that," he explained.

"You can have sex with her, I don't mind," Evelyn replied.

"Really? Like...you don't mind at all?"

"No. I'm not the jealous type, and...well, it kinda gets me hot, thinking about you fucking another hot chick."

"Seriously? That's fucking awesome," David said, sitting up a little straighter.

"Yeah." She shrugged. "I don't know. So, if at all possible, I want to watch you fucking Cait. Or anyone else we run into that catches your eye. And let me join in, if they're into that. I *love* girls. I think I do more than guys, honestly."

"Holy shit, you are going to be an amazing girlfriend."

She laughed. "I hope so." Then she became more serious. "Okay, so, we're dating. That's that settled. What about, um...everything else?"

He sighed and looked around the basement they had made their temporary home in. "Well, for the immediate future, we should probably stay here. We need to take inventory of anything on site and get at least *some* basics here and stored, to figure out what we're working with. Given the snow, I think we'll be good for water for a while, though it'd be great to have some way to store the boiled water.

"But we also need food and fire fuel at most minimum, plus any medical supplies and weapons to defend ourselves. So let's get up, get clean and dressed, eat breakfast, and then search this basement and the topside portion."

"Sounds like a plan," Evelyn said, and stood.

David blinked and stared up at her. She was like a goddess, or a giantess. She towered over him, an enormous visage of amazing beauty.

Yes, this was going to be a fucking *amazing* relationship.

...

They washed themselves up thoroughly.

For David, he did it both because of all the sweat and filth that had accumulated on him during all the frantic activity during last night, (the bad and the good), and to really help him focus. Because he was going to need it.

The situation was *pretty* fucked right now, and if

he and Evelyn were going to make it out of this situation alive, they were going to need to be sharp and hardworking. It already seemed obvious to him that Evelyn was both of these things, and he was definitely going to carry his own weight.

Once he was washed and dried, he located a dresser tucked away in one corner and dug through it. He needed his pack, his belongings. He managed to come up with enough clothes that fit to make most of an outfit, (he still pulled on his own cargo pants with all their pockets, as well as his jacket and heavy boots).

From there, they started hunting for breakfast.

David led the way up the stairs. He cautiously opened the door, pulling out his pistol. They hadn't brought any food with them, so they were going to have to either give up and go without for now, or just luck out hard. He was already starving, so here was to luck.

There didn't seem to be anything in the dilapidated room beyond, though there were drifts of snow from where it had gotten in. He no longer heard the shrieking of the winds, and the sunlight streaming in through the windows and holes looked clean and golden. Evelyn came up behind him. They crossed the room to the kitchen area and began hunting through cabinets and drawers and anywhere else there might be food.

In the end, they lucked out, though not by a whole lot.

The last cabinet they checked wasn't completely cleaned out. There were six cans there, each with a scrawl across them. Two were kidney beans, two were pears, two were chopped beef. There was also a gallon jug of clean-looking water in there. He took them all out, considering it, then looking at Evelyn.

"We should split it evenly," she said.

He shook his head. "No, that doesn't make sense. I know goliaths need more. I take two, you take four," he replied.

She frowned, looking guilty, then sighed. "Fine. What do you hate most?"

"Kidney beans, can't stand them," he replied.

She laughed. "I happen to love them, so that works out. Okay, let's eat."

They sat down on the floor beside each other and ate. David tore through both cans and drank off a quarter of the water. Evelyn finished off everything else. He felt decently confident that he could get at least some food from the ruined village.

A lot of people had died, and even the most motivated of survivors couldn't have searched the entire village by now. There was time. Although the sooner he got out there, the better.

In fact, that's what he almost suggested. But then he hesitated. There was a good chance there were still dangerous things hanging around. And there would be people excitedly rushing out there to get to the good stuff first. Why not let them deal with the creatures? He said as much to Evelyn, and she nodded in agreement.

"That makes sense. So now what?"

"Okay, how about you search the perimeter, make sure we're safe, and gather up whatever firewood and kindling you can, and I search in here for any more supplies that might be hidden away. Sound good?"

"Sounds great," she replied.

They got up, and she paused for a second, then she leaned down and kissed him on the lips. Then she giggled and straightened up. "This is making me really happy," she said.

"Me too," he replied, a big grin on his face. "Definitely very happy."

"Good luck, boyfriend."

"You too, girlfriend," he replied.

As she left, he couldn't help but feel a strange dissonance. He was undoubtedly in a horrific situation, what with the winter settling in and the village and the dangerous creatures everywhere. And yet, he was happier than he had been in a very, very long time.

Holding onto that feeling, he set to work.

. . .

The next three hours started out slow, then quickly seemed to pick up.

He'd hardly seen anything at all last night, as they'd pretty much just gone straight down to the basement. In fact, so much of last night was a blur. David still had the general gist of it, but everything after stepping out of his cabin was hazy and uncertain. In a way, he was glad. It had been a harrowing ordeal that he'd been lucky to survive.

All the close calls and terrifying moments...well, he'd rather just be happy that it was behind him and he'd gotten through it than remember and dwell on it.

There honestly wasn't much in the cabin.

There was a narrow bed in one corner, a table and some chairs near the fireplace, a dresser with a broken leg leaning heavily against the wall behind it, and finally the bathroom. He stepped inside and poked around through it, finding nothing at all. His search of the top floor turned up literally nothing of value beyond the furniture and that initial cache of food.

Well, at least the furniture could be burned if it came to that, though hopefully it wouldn't.

It was nice to have something to sit down on.

So then he took to the basement, which took longer to search than he'd hoped, because it was dark down there.

There were things crammed along the walls, mostly. Another old dresser, the one he'd searched to find his clothes, that had more clothes in it. A very old metal shelf with a bunch of junk on it, the kind of stuff that might be useful in the long term, he saw some tools and an old fan and a collection of hardback books, but weren't much use now.

There were a stack of old tires, again, maybe useful eventually, but not now. There was a big mirror. A collection of wooden chairs, a large stand-alone cupboard that had a bunch of old dishware in it, plates and silverware and cups, and mainly just boxes after that.

He sorted through it all, and ultimately found nothing of immediate value.

Anything of any real use was stuff that would've made for a great find to bring to a village and trade to people who could put it to use, and hey, there might be another village around here, possibly, but that was all in the near future. So he left the basement and went outside to find Evelyn.

He located her around back, dumping off a fresh batch of dead twigs and branches into a rather large pile behind the cabin, right next to a string of firewood.

There was even a hatchet resting in a little wooden enclosure attached to the back of the house.

Now *here* was something useful.

"Did you find anything?" she asked, dusting her hands together.

"No," he replied. "I mean, some clothes and tools and a few other things that we could trade, if we found someone to trade with, but otherwise nothing useful. What about you?"

"Just this," she replied, indicating the hatchet. "Although I *did* see like a campsite not far from here. It looked abandoned. I wanted to see if you'd be able to join me in checking it out."

"Definitely. Let's go now."

They set off.

"I think, after this, we should inventory what we have and then make for the village. I haven't heard any gunshots or shouts for a little while now, have you?"

"No, the last one I heard was almost an hour ago." She frowned. "It's likely going to be dangerous there..."

"Yeah, but we have to do it. It's going to be dangerous everywhere, realistically."

"Yeah," she agreed glumly.

The campsite turned out to be not very much, and it was a grim, grisly scene.

There were a pair of picnic tables, a barrel that had obviously been used to make a fire, the remnants of a few animals that had been hunted for meat and their skins, and a shredded, bloody tent. They spent about ten minutes picking over the site.

David very much doubted that whoever had been inside the tent had survived the attack, but the corpses weren't there. All he found was a severed hand. There was also a ripped open backpack, and a few scattered supplies.

They managed to salvage a few bottles of water, a not very big knife, and a magazine of ammo that fit David's pistol.

He still couldn't believe he'd held onto that, although the holster was missing and he was having to tuck it into his waistband. Not exactly comfortable. In the end, they left the campsite and headed back to the cabin.

"So...I guess we shouldn't put it off any longer, huh?" Evelyn asked as they circled around to the front and then hesitated.

David blew out a lengthy sigh. "Yeah..."

"Fuck. Let's get this over with then."

They began walking back the way they'd fled the night before.

...

It was actually nice out.

Although the storm had been brutal last night and had dumped several inches of snow on them, the sun was shining down, melting it all slowly, and it was probably in the low fifties. Not actually *great* weather, but a pretty good balance for being outside and working. He kept wary as they made their way through the forest.

Now that he was in the sunlight, he had a better sense of direction, and would probably be able to see the monsters coming. Probably. It depended on the creature, he supposed. But having Evelyn there *did* make things better.

"So...was it really that good?" Evelyn asked as they walked on.

"What?" he asked.

"Don't give me 'what?', you *know* 'what'."

"Oh. *That.* Yes, it was. It was amazing."

"Better than that girl you fucked before me?"

"I mean...overall, I think yeah. It wasn't undcr the best circumstances, but yeah, it felt really good. It felt...intimate."

"It did," she said, smiling fondly. "I really liked it." She paused, losing her smile. "If, um, if I get too...attached, or needy, or something like that, please tell me. I have a tendency to do that. It's caused problems in the past. So like, actually tell me if there's a problem, okay?"

"I will," he said, then wondered if there was anything he needed to worry about.

What tendencies did *he* have that might turn the relationship sour? He couldn't think of anything after a minute, but he figured that was largely because he just hadn't had all that many relationships. Or long-term relationships anyway, for obvious reasons.

"And, if anything *I'm* doing is bugging you, let me know, okay?"

"Okay," she agreed.

As he looked forward again, he frowned, seeing a thin haze of black smoke still rising into the air. Yes, they were definitely getting close to the village. A few moments later, they broke through a treeline. He could see the perimeter wall he'd had to jump last night.

It was partially collapsed now. They stood and listened for a minute, and when they didn't hear anything at all, they resumed their slow walk.

David went through first, pistol out, ready for anything.

He came to stand at the end of the main road that ran through town and bore witness to the devastation. At least half of the buildings had burned to nothing, and most of them had suffered some kind of fire damage. Two of them had collapsed.

And there were bodies everywhere.

Dozens of them, over a hundred probably. What a nightmare this was going to be.

But they couldn't afford to let the opportunity go to waste.

"Where to first?" Evelyn asked.

"My shack," he replied. "I want to see if my pack is still there."

"Good idea."

The shack he'd rented was nearby and looked intact. He walked slowly up to it. The door was open, and he couldn't remember if he'd closed it behind him. Probably not. He peered slowly inside, and frowned at what he saw. The place was tossed, his personal effects, those that remained, scattered across the floor.

"Crap," he muttered. "I'll check in here, why don't you check the next shack?"

"On it," Evelyn replied, and moved over to it.

His clothes had mostly been left alone, which was nice. And they hadn't actually taken his backpack, just dumped it. He stuffed his clothing back into the pack, as well as a few paperback novels that had survived, and, after a more thorough search, he managed to find a bottle of water and two cans of chopped chicken that had rolled under his bed.

Everything else had been stolen.

With a sigh, he shrugged into his pack and stepped back outside.

There was a lot of work scavenging and trading and earning and hunting just gone. David didn't let it get to him, or he tried not to, anyway. He'd had massive setbacks before. Hell, he'd lost everything before. It was just...it wore thin after the tenth time. Although he had to admit it was easier to push back against whcn he was surrounded by so much devastation and destruction.

And corpses.

There were dozens of people here who had lost it *all*.

And having Evelyn around helped.

Just knowing she was nearby made a big positive impact on his mood. As he moved over to another nearby shack and began to search it for supplies, he found himself wondering about that. Was it just because she was going to be dangerous to anyone who wanted to hurt him? No, he didn't think so. There *was* a certain animal comfort in knowing you had another person around to help you in case of danger, but this went beyond that.

Was it because he'd had sex with her, and was going to again? That was closer, and the thought of it sent a little zap of lust into him, but that wasn't it either.

Maybe it was because he just liked her.

Fast-forming relationships were commonplace nowadays, and it was more common than ever over the past year, what with the sudden appearance of all the new zombie monsters.

But that was almost always born out of a shared desire for comfort and safety. You met someone, you sparked violently, you have crazy sex for a few days, and then it began to wear off and if they were still around, you started to get a good look at the person you'd hooked up with.

And more often than not, found that you didn't really like them nearly as much as you thought you did. But that wasn't happening with Evelyn. He *really* liked her.

It had been over a week now, which was a pretty long time by current standards, and there was just this *feeling*. It was hard to describe, but it was like...they'd been together for a long time. Like they were already familiar with each other. It was a deeply comforting feeling. It scared him, in a way, because the more you cared about someone, the more it hurt when they were ripped away from you.

And that was a major threat, even worse in the conditions they presently found themselves in. Well, he supposed he was just going to have to be better, fight harder, focus more. He cared about Evelyn. It had been a long time since he'd really cared about anything.

It was a great feeling.

He found a few cans of food in the shack and slipped them into his pack, then rejoined Evelyn, who had finished searching the other two shacks.

"Anything?"

"A pistol, a combat knife, a sewing kit," she replied.

"Not bad." He turned and looked at the ruin of the village and his shoulders slumped a little. This was going to be a long fucking day. "Let's get to work."

. . .

It was a slow, bad day.

The more they searched, the more obvious it was that people had already come and gone. Whole buildings were cleared out. An hour passed, then two, then three whole hours. They both got sweaty and irritable and then cold and more irritable.

Although it wasn't a *total* waste, as they'd managed to pack Evelyn's backpack with many cans of food and also had come across a bit of ammunition, it was far less than David had been hoping for. He felt like kicking himself.

He should have marched over here first thing in the morning.

But then, fuck, he'd probably have gotten himself killed. Either by the zombies still lurking around, or whoever had come to loot the place. There was a good chance that it was those thieves who'd caused the whole mess in the first place.

Right about the time their fourth hour was coming to a close, they made a big discovery.

"Wait," David said, freezing, "did you hear that?"

Evelyn stopped moving. They were near the middle of the village, not far from a partially collapsed apartment building. They'd debated going into it, and ultimately decided against it, given it was too structurally unsound to be worth it.

"No–" Evelyn began, but David shushed her.

There. A soft moan.

"Okay, I heard that," she whispered. "A zombie?"

"I don't think so..."

David moved closer to the source of the sound: the half collapsed building. He walked up to a smashed window and listened. A few seconds passed. A cold wind blew. The moan sounded again, less faint.

"It's definitely coming from in here, and I don't think it's a zombie. It sounds like pain, not like mindless hunger."

"It's too dangerous to go in there..." Evelyn said

uncertainly.

"We can't leave them," he replied. "Stay here, okay? Watch my back."

"I...fuck, okay. Just *please* be careful, David."

"I will," he promised.

He stepped up to the window and peered in. Someone had obviously gone in already, as the frame had been cleared of glass shards, for the most part. It would be dangerous in there. With a sigh, David forced himself onward.

He slipped carefully in through the opening, and found himself standing in someone's bedroom. It had been tossed, so looters had come in here, too. Hopefully they were long gone. And hopefully he wasn't trying to rescue one of the people who'd burned half this fucking village to the ground.

He pulled out his pistol and lighter, lit it, then set off.

"Hello!?" he called as he stepped out of the bedroom and into a living room.

Nothing. He waited, standing there for nearly thirty seconds, before finally moving on again. Maybe they'd passed out. Or died. Fuck, what a shitty situation. He checked out the apartment, which didn't take long, given how small it was, then stepped out into the hallway beyond.

It was a mess. Halfway down to his right was a lot of cave-in.

"Hello!? Can you hear me!?" he yelled.

The moan again, and he thought there might've been a word in there that sounded vaguely like *help*. And...of course it was coming from the direction of the cave-in. David walked slowly up to it, eyeing it cautiously, and saw that there was a narrow gap near the floor. He could, if pressed, wriggle through there.

"Fuck me," he whispered, and, after a moment's consideration, holstered his pistol and got down on his hands and knees.

It took way too long, and left him with several painful scrapes, but eventually David wormed his way through to the other side. As he got slowly back to his feet, coughing a few times from the dust in the air, he saw that it was pretty bad on this side. It was obvious that the left side of the building was just fucked, judging from the bulging walls and beams and pieces of rebar and concrete breaking through in some places.

The other side, however, was not.

And that was where the moaning was coming from, he surmised, hearing it again.

"I'm coming!" he called, and moved over to the second apartment on the right side. He opened the door and stepped into the living room, looking around. There! A figure lying among the rubble, well, more like curled up in the corner with a tattered blanket thrown over her.

He moved over to her. "Hey, I'm here," he said.

The person shifted slightly, but otherwise didn't react.

Shit, was this a trap of some kind?

"Can you hear me?" he asked, raising the lighter higher and looking around. He didn't see or sense anyone else in the room, and the only other door out of there was buckled outward, indicating another cave-in. "Hello?"

A soft moan. "Help..."

David saw a green, scaly tail poking out from beneath the blanket. The voice was feminine. He moved over, crouched, and gently pulled back the blanket. He discovered a petite rep woman in a torn dress curled up, shivering.

Oh shit, that's right, they were cold-blooded. They did horribly in cold environments. And he could see his breath in here.

She had several scrapes and cuts, and what looked like a bad blow to the head.

"Holy shit, don't worry, I'm going to get you out of here," he said, and put away his lighter.

It was dark, but not pitch-black, as the sun was coming in through a few holes in the walls and ceiling. It was brightest back the way he'd come. He scooped her up in his arms and stood. She didn't weigh all that much. Carefully, he carried her back across the room, trying not to fall.

"Can you hear me? What's your name?" he asked softly.

Nothing. She was still breathing, but she was out, definitely.

Fuck, had to get her warm and fast.

It was a bit of a pain in the ass, okay, a massive one, but he managed to get her through the opening as carefully as he could, having to mainly drag her through it, wincing each time he pulled. He was glad she was out for this part, because it would no doubt be painful, but at the moment he didn't see any other way.

Once she was through, he picked her back up and carried her through the apartment, to the window where Evelyn was waiting.

"Oh my God, who's this?" she asked.

"No idea, I found her in another apartment. We have to get her warm right now."

"Here, give her to me."

Evelyn stuck her arms in through the window, and he passed her carefully to the goliath, who lifted her easily through the window and cradled her gently in her huge arms. David hopped through as Evelyn stepped back to make room.

"Where should we go?" she asked.

David began to respond, thinking they should get back to his shack to temporarily get her warmed up, but he heard a growl from somewhere nearby.

And then several more responded.

"Fuck," he snapped. "We have to get her out of here, back to the cabin."

They hurried off, heading rapidly out of the ruined village.

# CHAPTER FIVE

Although they made good time getting back to their temporary homestead, it still felt like far too long. The poor woman was shivering violently now that she was actually outside. David threw his coat over her prone form, but doubted it helped all that much.

Once they arrived, he quickly cleared the area around the cabin, then the first floor, then the basement, making sure nothing had gotten in during their absence. Once that task was dealt with, they got the woman into the basement and laid her in the nest of blankets, then restarted the fire after getting her bundled up.

"We don't have any medicine of any kind," Evelyn muttered as she took a bottle of water and a washcloth, and began to gently wipe away the woman's head wound.

"No, we don't," David replied, thinking furiously. "Fuck, where would some be..."

"That abandoned campground," Evelyn said, looking up at him suddenly.

"What abandoned campground? The one we searched already?"

"No, no, a camp*ground,* not a campsite. Like, a bunch of buildings in a fenced in area...fuck, I forgot, you weren't there. One of the jobs I took early on while you were busy one day was to go looking for someone who'd gone missing, they'd been checking out those campgrounds. I found them there and they were under attack. We had to get out of there fast, but I think there might be some supplies there. If you head northwest from here, you should be able to find it."

"Fuck, that's a big if," he muttered.

"I know, but it's that or search the area blindly or go back to the village..."

"Yeah, you're right. Shit, okay, I'll get to it. You have to stay here and make sure nothing happens to her, though."

She nodded morosely. "Please be careful, David. I...don't want to lose you."

"I'll be careful, Evelyn," he replied, and he gave her a long, lingering kiss on the mouth.

After that, David emptied his pack of all but the most necessary supplies, given he might run into other things out there, and he did need to unload what he'd found in the ruined village. Once that was done, he headed out once more into the cold.

...

He walked for maybe twenty minutes, using the sun, inasmuch as he could, to guide him.

He tried not to let doubt gnaw at him, but that was a difficult prospect. Besides the fact that he could get lost out here, and besides the fact that someone was relying on him, he was more paranoid than ever about the monsters that roamed the landscape.

When you went long enough without encountering one, it was surprisingly easy to forget how dangerous and deadly they were. But after an experience like the one at the village the previous night, well...he was more cognizant than ever of just how lethal the hideous mutations roaming the countryside were.

Right about the time he was really beginning to worry, he crested a small rise in the land and suddenly found himself looking at exactly what Evelyn had described to him: a campground. He spotted about a dozen buildings, mostly cabins, surrounded by a twelve-foot mesh-wire fence that was still surprisingly intact.

As he approached it, he wondered why no one was living here. It would make a pretty great base of operations.

He entered through the main entrance and looked around. There was a central sort of road going to the left and right of his current position, with a row of structures on either side. Walking forward, he passed between two cabins that had a pathway leading from the main entrance between them, and came to stand in the center of the camp.

He sized the place up. Ahead of him were six cabins in a row, with another pair of cabins at the end of the road to the right, and then on the other side of the road, now to his back, were four more cabins.

Completing it all at the left end of the road was another big, three-story structure that looked like it might have once housed management or something.

That seemed like a good place to start. However, as he began to head for it, he heard a low, gruff growl. Cursing, he pulled out his pistol. From in between two of the cabins ahead of him, a human zombie stepped out.

David aimed and fired. The shot was good, taking it in the forehead and putting it down with ease. Unfortunately, the loud gunshot signaled the onset of a dozen more zombies. They began drifting out into the main road from between the cabins.

Fuck. David took aim and fired off another shot, dropping a second zombie. Then a third, and a fourth. The muzzle flashed and the gun jumped in his grasp.

Even now, with them faster and deadlier, they were still relatively easy to kill. It was just a problem when they crowded in on you, and usually there were a lot of them. He'd killed eight of them when he caught sight of a stalker.

"Oh fuck me," he whispered, whipping the gun in that direction and backing away, towards a hole he'd cleared for himself among them.

The stalker, a lean, mean horror with way too long, razor sharp claws and a tendency to blend into its surroundings, was coming for him fast. He swallowed, aiming at it, focusing on it to the exclusion of everything else.

He had to kill this thing now before it murdered him, and it would.

Very quickly and very painfully.

David kept a bead on it, then squeezed the trigger. The first shot missed. He cursed and fired again. The second bullet clipped it, sent it stumbling. It crashed to the ground. He hastily readjusted him aim and popped off a third shot.

That did it: one straight to the face, piercing its brain and killing it. It went slack.

Then a zombie he'd lost focus of got ahold of his left arm.

David yelled and jerked, but the bastard wouldn't let go. He shoved the pistol into its mouth and pulled the trigger. It killed the zombie, but the thing had a death grip and took him down with it. He cried out in surprise as he was yanked down, then in pain as he hit the ground. The remaining zombies were fast approaching.

With no time to get up, he took aim and resumed fire. A few shots later his gun ran dry and he hastily reloaded, then finished them off.

When no more came, he took a deep breath and let it out slowly, then got to his feet and looked around the campground, which was now a field of death. Well, at least there was a lot for him to do. But that just made him think of the poor woman he'd found injured and half-frozen suffering back at the ramshackle place he and Evelyn were calling their home.

Feeling a strong motivation coming over him, he holstered his pistol, and hastily set to work searching the bodies. He doubted any of them were carrying medicine, but you never knew.

It took a quarter of an hour to search all the corpses, and he at least managed to find a few good things for his trouble.

A switchblade, a lighter, a little pocket toolkit with some screwdrivers and other tools someone could use.

No medicine though, not even painkillers. Growing frustrated, he set to work searching the cabins, and all in all, it took him less time than he thought it would. Although it still felt like too much. The main reason for this was because several of them were totally, completely empty. They'd been utterly cleared out even of furniture.

David felt a rising frustration as he finished his search of the final structure, the main office, and came to stand back out in the corpse-strewn road between the cabins. He told himself to relax, this was honestly to be expected, given how long these structures had probably stood here. But there was the rep to think about, and it honestly didn't help that reality was the way it was. If anything, it induced more stress, because it made his chances worse

But he abruptly left the camp the way he'd come

in, making a mental note to come back here.

It was a solid location, certainly more secure than their present home site.

Might be a good idea to move.

He'd caught sight of something between the cabins during his search: a road. Like a real paved road, between the trees, leading roughly north-south. Maybe it led somewhere. Unfortunately, right now, that flimsy logic was about all he had to go on. So he marched over, through the trees, and hit the road. Looking down either length, he saw that he had it to himself, for now at least.

Intent on finding *something*, he began walking at a brisk pace.

...

A mountain that he had noticed when first coming in and had often captivated him whenever he caught sight of it now dominated his view.

He'd been walking along the road for a good twenty minutes now. Mountains always awed him. There was something humbling in their enormity and sheer bulk, and natural beauty. Staring at the way the land swept up, this particular mountain covered in a thick blanket of trees, was breathtaking.

High up, he could see what looked like the rusted remains of an ancient radio tower.

He wondered when the last time a living thing had been up there.

Finally, he found a building.

He'd passed three cars on the way in, but they were stripped-down, skeletal husks with nothing of any real value left, unless he was looking for rusted metal. Everything of any actual value had long since been looted.

The structure he came to was a broad, slate gray brick of corrugated metal. He figured it to be a two-story warehouse and thought that there was probably a decent chance that someone had at one point used it as a place to get in out of bad weather. Now, whether or not they'd left anything behind, or were still lingering, those were other questions.

And then there were other possibilities…

Like more lethal inhabitants.

David walked down a short, gravel road that led off the main one, then across a parking lot with just a single burned-out wreck sitting in it. His boots crunched in the snow and gravel as he approached the main entrance.

This was potentially going to be extremely dangerous. But what recourse did he have? Besides the village, he didn't know of anything around. But as he approached, he paused, catching sight of something else.

It was to the right of the warehouse, deeper into the woods surrounding the structure.

A watchtower of some kind.

Well, if this didn't work out, then it was his next stop.

David got to the door and tried the handle. It wasn't locked. Carefully, he pushed the door open and peered inside. He had a view of about half the main interior, the right side. His view of the left was blocked mostly by an enormous stack of shipping containers that extended to the halfway mark of the warehouse.

As he stepped inside, leaving the door open, he scoped out the area. The sunlight filtered in through dirty windows up above, bathing the warehouse in a murky gloom. But something glinted up high, on the second story.

A wall-mounted medical station!

One of those little metal boxes painted red with a white plus symbol on it. People still stocked them with medicine sometimes! Was it intact? It was closed, at least, he could see that much, and he *thought* he could see the bulb of a little padlock that some of them used to keep them secure, but that might just be wishful thinking.

David had good vision, but even it was being tested in this low light level. He looked around the warehouse. From what he could see, he had the place to himself, but that might not be totally accurate.

Immediately to his right was a metal staircase leading up to a pathway granting access to the second story. He could be up there and at it in under sixty seconds. This felt like too good an opportunity to pass up, so, moving as fast as he could while still being careful, he slipped along the wall and up the stairs.

Okay, this could work. This could really work.

In his head, David saw himself opening the case, finding medical supplies, slipping back outside, and hurrying home. It all seemed so wonderfully plausible.

Then he reached the top, and made the mistake of looking out over the warehouse proper. Something caught his eye and it sent up warning flags. He hesitated, now standing at the top of the stairs, on the second story walkway, and stared harder.

There were...shapes.

Deeper in the warehouse, in a large section of open space that had been hidden from view when he'd first come in. As he watched, one of them shifted slightly.

The reality of his situation came crashing down on him with all the force of a point blank shotgun blast. Those were creatures. He didn't know what kind they were, but he knew they were dangerous, and would murder him if they woke up.

"*Fuck me,*" he whispered, trying to control the terror that was currently threatening to overwhelm his body.

A very strong piece of him wanted to just bolt, just dead sprint right back down the stairwell and out the way he'd come in. But not only would that be suicide, he'd leave without the medicine. He didn't know if it was up there, but he had to try. Taking a deep breath, he let it out very slowly, trying to count them.

He stopped at a dozen.

Too many, that's how many were in there with him.

Jesus fucking shit. He slowly turned to face the open doorway that had the wall-mounted kit. It was perhaps ten feet away from his present position. He could be there, even at a slow pace, in less than half a minute.

He looked back down to the creatures. They were immobile lumps, for the most part, passed out. David gathered up his courage, whatever he could manage, and then turned away from them. He began to make slow, steady progress across the walkway.

It felt like roughly thirty minutes, instead of thirty seconds, but he finally managed to make it to his destination. He'd been tossing glances at the creatures again and again, and he did so once more as he stepped into the doorway. They had yet to move. He let out a gentle sigh and stepped slowly into the room.

He'd viewed the kit through a hole in the wall where a window had once been, and imagined this had, decades ago, been a manager's office perhaps. There was a desk at the back of the room. He moved over to the metal box.

*Oh thank fuck,* he thought, seeing that there was indeed a tiny padlock on it.

He pulled on it, found it locked, and reached into his pocket. One of the things he carried with him was a small pair of bolt-cutters. They couldn't deal with the heavy-duty padlocks, but they could get through something like this. Producing the cutters, he set to work. It took a little bit to get through, as his cutters weren't as sharp as they used to be, but finally he cut the lock.

Carefully extracting it, he set it on top of the housing and then pulled the little door open.

Jack-fucking-pot.

There was a store of medical supplies. He wouldn't quite call it a treasure trove or the motherlode, but under the present circumstances, it should be more than enough. There were bandages, antiseptic injections and bottles, painkillers, suture kits, a thermometer, gauze, and several other things he couldn't readily identify but knew would be useful.

David spent a moment shrugging out of his pack and then carefully transferring everything into it. He tried to position it so that nothing would shift around or clink together too much.

When he was done, he looked hesitantly around the office. There was a chance this was the only thing useful in the whole building, but...well, it had been a long-shot that this would be here and intact, and it had paid off, so he was really wanting to continue his search.

But this was far, far too dangerous. He had to get out while the getting was good. With that in mind, David crept back over to the stairwell. As he reached it and placed his foot on the first step, the metal walkway shifted beneath him, and a loud, metallic groan filled the air.

He waited, terrified that it was going to collapse beneath him.

It held, but it had a just as bad effect: all of the creatures in the area were now awake. And they were all looking at him.

"Oh fuck," he whispered, and pulled out his pistol.

The nearest one cut loose with a low, rumbling growl, and he knew that he was dealing with wildcats. They were jags who had been turned by the new virus. And they were *fast* and fucking *dangerous*. And his odds of getting out of this one were not good. The nearest one was stalking slowly forward, staring up at him.

David recalled what he knew about the wildcats. They were ferocious, and they tended to leap quite well, and could run like hell. The first one came into the light and he found himself staring at a lean, limber figure covered in a patchwork of fur. Its ropy musculature bulged beneath its rotting flesh.

He aimed and fired.

The bullet punched through the thing's skull, killing it, but it was like a starting pistol for the rest of them.

The only good news was that they would be forced to go up the stairwell when coming at him. He *might* have a chance with a bottleneck like that. And so he set to the task of keeping his ass alive. He kept his hands as steady as he could, and at first, it worked.

He killed another one, and then popped the skull of a third, before the others began to hit the stairwell. And he killed another, and another, and tripped up the others.

And he felt like he was actually going to survive this mess.

That was precisely the moment the walkway began shuddering rapidly, and he heard running footsteps, and David threw a glance to his right and screamed. Three of them had somehow gotten up farther down the walkway! Even as he readjusted his aim and began punching hot lead into their rotting bodies, he saw two more scrambling up a pile of crates.

Dammit! They were closing in too fast, now from two sides.

Several things happened at once, then.

He heard shattering glass. He heard gunfire.

One of the wildcats to his right, approaching rapidly from the walkway, went down with the back of its head blown out. Then a second one went down. He saw muzzle flare coming from up above, through one of the skylights.

Someone was saving his ass, apparently.

Cait?

No time for that now. He returned his attention to the ones coming up the stairs, hastily reloaded, and began putting them down. It was relatively easy to focus again now that he knew someone was helping him out. Within ten seconds they were all dead, and the warehouse fell silent again.

Breathing heavily, he holstered his pistol and took a few steps closer to his mysterious savior. They stood silhouetted against the winter sun in one of the skylights. He could see...a feminine figure, but it was hard to tell otherwise.

"Cait!?" he called.

"No," a sharp reply came. As he drew closer, he saw a few more features: a tail, fur. So a jag had saved him.

The woman suddenly turned to go. "Wait!" he cried.

She hesitated. "What?"

"I, um...thank you. And, I could use some help. I'm from River View. It was destroyed last night. Myself and two other survivors are holed up right now, and one of them is injured."

A brief pause, then: "No. Don't follow me."

"Wait!" he called, but she was gone.

He sighed softly. Well, he figured, looking around at all the bodies, he was lucky. Damn lucky. And this is what ultimately decided him when he again felt the urge to stick around and hunt for more useful items. It wasn't the time to push his luck.

David began making his way down the stairs, back to the light.

...

"David," Evelyn said, sounding deeply relieved as he came into the topside of their cabin. She had found a broom somewhere and was in the process of sweeping up. The place looked neater, and she'd pushed a dresser in front of one of the broken windows. "Are you okay?"

"Yeah. Had a really close call, but I got the meds," he replied.

"Oh thank God," she whispered.

"Is she okay?"

"Yes. She came around a few times, and I think she's finally latched onto the notion that she's somewhere safe, and we're taking care of her. Her wounds don't seem that bad, actually, though I still want to get her patched up. I think her biggest problems are the cold and dehydration. So I've been giving her water. She's drained two bottles so far. Come on, let's get her fixed up," she said, setting the broom aside and crossing to the door leading to the basement. He followed after her, then she hesitated and turned to face him again.

She hugged him suddenly. "You did really good, and I'm so glad you're safe."

"Thank you, and so am I," he replied, grinning despite everything that had happened. "I was rescued," he added.

"By who? What actually happened?"

He brought her up to speed as they headed downstairs. The woman was still passed out, but she was no longer curled up in a ball beneath the blankets. She was lying on her side, blankets pulled up around her, head resting on a few pillows.

The fire still burned mellowly. It was pleasantly warm in the basement. David got out of his pack and began unloading the medical supplies on a desk pressed up against the wall.

"I was thinking about rearranging some of this," Evelyn said, "maybe making it a little more livable, you know? Unless you think that'd be a waste of time."

"I think it's a great idea," he replied, finishing up. "I was thinking–"

They both froze as they heard a thump from upstairs.

The pair stared intently at each other, then David

pulled out his pistol and slipped over to the stairs. He crept up them, tensing up immediately, and got to the door. He waited, listening. Another thump. Someone, or something, was walking around out there. Carefully, he reached out, gripped the knob, twisted it gently, and slowly opened the door.

The above ground portion of the cabin was gradually revealed. He saw a shadow moving around at first, and immediately knew it was something undead.

He licked his lips and raised the pistol, waiting.

A zombie wandered into view. He aimed and fired. As he did, something shrieked wildly and leaped into view. A stalker! Fuck! He aimed and fired, missed, fired, missed again, and in his panic, emptied his pistol.

He managed to put a shot through its face and killed it, but felt angry and embarrassed that he'd missed that many times at goddamned point blank!

"Fuck," he hissed as he reloaded.

"Are you okay?" Evelyn asked.

"I'm fine. I think we're clear. I'm heading out," he replied.

"I'll join you."

They went into the topside portion together and took a few minutes to search the area. The zombies had gotten in through one of the open windows.

"We've got to patch these up," David muttered. "But that's not our biggest problem right now."

"What is?" Evelyn asked.

"We need more ammo. And something more than pistols. I mean, if we intend to survive for any real length of time." He paused, thinking about it. "I guess I could go back to the warehouse..."

"Wait, David, um, I remembered something else.

Another place we could go to search. The road we initially came in on, there's three buildings farther on down them, at a crossroads."

David sighed, suddenly remembering what she was talking about.

"I'm sorry I didn't remember it earlier...are you mad?"

"No. I mean, I'm annoyed, but annoyed that *I* didn't remember them."

"It's been a stressful day."

He laughed softly. "Yeah, it definitely has." He took a deep breath and let it out slowly, then reached up and rubbed the back of his neck. "I guess I should head out."

"I should go this time," Evelyn said.

"No, I want you to stay here and protect this place," he replied. It was a testament to how much she really didn't want to go out that she didn't argue.

"Okay," she murmured softly.

He moved over and hugged her again, then she leaned down and gave him a long kiss. "I'll be careful," he said.

# CHAPTER SIX

David calculated that he had maybe two hours of light left in the day.

That *should* be enough to get out there, search the buildings, hopefully find something worthwhile, then head back.

He found himself frustrated as he roved out from the abandoned cabin. (Well, he supposed it wasn't abandoned any longer.) He should have remembered that, but he supposed he should give himself the same pass he'd given Evelyn, because it was true: they'd both been too exhausted, too harrowed from the night before, for their brains to work properly.

Still, he felt stupid and angry at himself.

But that slowly wore off as he moved through the woods, found the same, long road he and Evelyn had initially met and walked in on, and got walking. Instead, he found himself thinking of the jag woman who had saved his ass.

He was able to piece a few things together about her just from that simple encounter, like she was probably very competent, she was obviously an excellent shot, she cared about people, or at least enough to save his ass.

Who was she? Someone that was just passing through? A native to the region?

They could really use the help of someone like that.

He pushed at that thought, because it led him to wondering what their chances of survival were. And they felt not very good. David thought he had gotten pretty good at keeping a level head about staying alive, about living in a world fraught with danger, and he supposed he had, looking back on it. He'd grown up decades after the world had already collapsed and reformed around the threat of the zombies.

But all that was different now, it was much worse.

And now he would be lucky if he lived long enough to readjust his thinking and survival tactics to make it through this horrible new world.

In this spirit, David kept a sharp eye out as he marched down one side of the road, looking for threats, the human, inhuman, and monster variety. The only thing he saw of any real interest was a river that ran alongside the road. It had started some miles back, and it had been pleasant to walk alongside.

He wondered how many people were fishing in it, as that was a good potential food source.

Although squids, the inhumans who had adapted to live underwater, might live in it, or where it finally let out into. He thought that Cait had mentioned a lake somewhere in the area. David refocused as he saw the three buildings up ahead. He remembered them now. He and Evelyn had been on a patrol their second day in the village, agreeing to take the job in exchange for a pair of meals each, and they'd seen the buildings from a distance.

Now it was time to check them over. David severely doubted anything would be left.

But you never knew.

His theory about *everyone* thinking the same thing, and thus no one coming to check, had held water last time, in the warehouse. Maybe it would here, too. From what he could see, one of the structures had once been a gasoline station, another appeared to have been a garage, and if he had to guess, he'd say the third had been perhaps a restaurant.

But it was difficult to discern with how weathered and old they were. The garage was the nearest one, so that was where he started. David walked slowly up to it, trying to look in through the windows, but it looked like something was covering most of them from inside.

Maybe a blanket or a–

The front door opened up and a grim man holding a pistol stepped out. "That's close enough," he said flatly, raising the pistol.

David froze, his heart hammering. "I'm, uh, I'm not here for any trouble," he said.

"You should leave," the man replied.

"Please...do you have any ammo to trade? Guns? I'm from the village that fell yesterday..."

The man stared at him, his eyes flat and unreadable, but he seemed to be calculating something, trying to determine if this was some kind of trap or not.

David had seen people act like this before. The man was thin and wiry, his head and face covered in a thin layer of dark stubble streaked with gray. He looked desperate, but anxious in a familiar kind of way...he wasn't alone, David realized at once. Something about the way he was standing, the subtle undercurrent of fear and desperation in his voice.

Slowly, he lowered the pistol a bit.

David saw movement behind him, from the darkness beyond the doorway he stood in, and a pale, small face appeared at his side. The man glanced down sharply, then sighed. "Goddamnit, Allison, I said stay in the back!" he whispered harshly.

"I want to see if it's Ben," the little girl said.

She couldn't have been more than five or six.

David felt something tear at his heart.

"I'm really not going to cause problems, and I'm alone right now. We really just need some ammo, we're running low," David said. "I'd be willing to negotiate."

The man, who had shifted to stand in front of the girl, finally lowered the pistol all the way.

He sighed. "We were from the village too," he muttered. "I wasn't sure if anyone else made it out of that nightmare." He frowned, then holstered the pistol and reached up, rubbing his jaw. His eyes went to the other two structures. "Okay, I'll make you a deal. We've been hearing noises all night from the gas station next door. What does your pistol take?"

"Nine millimeter," David replied.

"I'll give you two magazines for it now if you agree to clear out those other two buildings, and I'll give you some more ammo if you agree to get us some food and medicine. We..." he hesitated, no doubt wondering how much information he should give away, "...we really need food," he finished finally.

"I accept," David replied, because fuck, he felt bad for these people. "How many are you?" he asked as he slowly approached.

The man said something over his shoulder, glancing back briefly, and then the little girl disappeared, probably taken back to safety by her mother. The man returned his attention to David, who stood a few feet away, keeping his movements calm and slow.

"There's four of us, my wife, my daughter, and another survivor who we ran into. A teenager who was alone," he said. "What about you?"

"I just have two others back in the cabin we're

staying in. A goliath, you might've seen her around, and a rep woman we found back in the village."

"You went back?" the man asked.

"Yeah, figured there'd be supplies there."

"Were there?"

David sighed. "Not as much as I'd have liked. Obviously someone got there first."

"Fuckers," the man growled. "If I ever find the pieces of garbage who attacked the village..." He looked genuinely pissed, and David knew how he felt.

It took a special kind of evil to do what those monsters had done last night.

God, last night. It felt like the attack was last week already.

Someone briefly appeared behind the man again and gave him something. Two magazines. He held them out. David walked up and accepted them.

The man offered his hand. "Jim Carlson," he said.

David pocketed the magazines, then shook his hand. "David Hunter."

Jim uttered a small laugh. "Not a half-bad name."

"Thanks. I'll be back as soon as I can and see what I can do about finding any food or medicine," he said.

"I really appreciate it. I was preparing to do it myself, but...I hate leaving them alone."

"I understand."

David left him and the man shut and locked the door firmly. Well, that had gone better than he'd hoped. Now came the hard part.

The gas station was up first, as per the request, and he studied it intently as he made a slow approach. Most of the windows were broken out, and the bleak sunlight lit the interior decently. He couldn't see anything, but that didn't mean it was safe. He hopped lightly through the window and looked around to make sure nothing was lurking in the immediate area, then began moving slowly around the interior.

There were definitely shadowy places along the L-shaped gas station, with him being at the 'top' of the L, and the rest of it disappearing from view at the opposite end and to the right. There were shelves, all of them bare and corroded, taking up most of the space. He checked them out, moving carefully among them, and found nothing.

Slowly, he approached the turn in the building, then peered around it. The only place anything could be hiding was behind a counter at the back of the area.

He considered it for a moment.

He couldn't see anything, and heard nothing, but some of these new types were *extremely* stealthy. Finally, he moved slowly out into the open space in front of the counter. Maybe he could lure it out, if anything was even back there, and–

A dark blur appeared, bounded up onto the counter, and launched itself at him all in the bare space of perhaps a second and a half. He screamed and began firing, shock and terror flooding his system. There was a shriek and his legs went out from under him. He saw blood fly, and then the creature, it was a stalker he realized, sailed over him.

Jittery and hyped up on adrenaline, he rolled over and tried to track it.

He'd hit it twice, and done some damage. It hit the floor a few feet behind where he'd been standing and began scrabbling to come after him. He kept firing, pounding out four more rounds before one connected with its misshapen head and killed it, spraying its rotted brains all over the area behind it. David slowly let out a sigh.

"Fuck me," he whispered, "too close."

After the adrenaline passed, he shakily got to his feet, then took the opportunity to double-check behind the counter. He pulled out his flashlight and shined it into the dark niches beneath the counter and among the shelves at the back.

"Oh shit," he whispered.

There was a milk crate shoved back up into the space beneath one of the large shelves attached to the walls behind the counter. He pulled it out, hoping against hope, and was rewarded for his efforts.

The thing was packed with cans.

He shrugged out of his pack and transferred a dozen and a half cans of food, as well as a can-opener, and four tins of sardines. It sure made his pack heavy, but given that he'd emptied out everything else, it was manageable. He finished his search of the area, found nothing more, and returned to the stark winter sunshine.

From there, it was a simple prospect of crossing the street and entering the final structure, which did indeed turn out to have once been a restaurant. Not that that meant anything anymore.

He found a pair of zombies milling about and shot them both through the head, then performed a thorough search. Unfortunately, all this one turned up was a can of vegetable soup laying forgotten at the back of a cabinet.

Well, that was two thirds of his problem solved. He marched back over to the garage and knocked on the door. It opened a few seconds later.

"I heard gunshots," Jim said.

"There was a stalker over in the gas station, and a

few zombies in the restaurant, but they're dead now. And I managed to hit a little jackpot," David replied, setting his pack down and opening it up.

Jim looked inside. "Holy crap, that's a good haul," he murmured.

"Yep. Here."

He gave them all the sardines, the can-opener, and all but three of the cans, figuring he deserved at least some of it for his trouble. If Jim disagreed, he didn't say anything. He just accepted the cans and passed them back to a pale woman with long dark hair and his daughter, who both took them deeper into the garage.

"No medicine then?" he asked when David zipped back up his pack and pulled it back on.

"Not yet," David replied. "Do you know of any other buildings in the area?"

"Well, there's a little side road a bit further down the way, but...this is a decent trade. If you want, we could call it even," he said uncertainly.

"No," David replied, "we had a deal. I'll get you some medicine."

"I...thank you," Jim said, looking relieved.

He wondered if one of them was sick, or beginning to show signs.

"I'll be back."

"We'll be here."

David left them again, picking back up his path and walking along the side of the road, hunting for that side path Jim had mentioned.

Despite everything, he felt good. He was helping people.

That just...felt good.

In as simple, plain, blunt a way as anything felt, it was a positive feeling. A moment later, he'd found the road he was looking for and began moving down it. Not too far away he saw a house among the dead and dying trees.

All around him, snow melted in the sun. It was a unique kind of time, that period after the first initial big snowfall, and then the calm that tended to follow. He wondered how long of a reprieve they would get. It could be a week, or days, or there might be a blizzard tonight. He hated how unpredictable the weather was.

And it was a far more desperate situation now than before. David kept this in mind as he scrutinized the house he was approaching. It was a simple, single-story building, not very large, derelict.

The garage door was open, and looked like it had rusted that way, so that was the way he went in. Pistol out, he decided to clear the house first. If he didn't find any medication here, then he'd go back and give at least some of what he'd found at the warehouse to the people. The garage was empty. The door at the back was open. He moved slowly through it and–

"Fuck!"

An explosion of pain burst into being and brilliant, blinding white washed across his vision. He stumbled, tripped over his own feet, and collapsed to the hard floor with a harsh grunt. This was it. He was dead.

Someone was attacking him and he'd stupidly walked into it.

"Oh fuck, it's you," he heard a vaguely familiar voice say.

The attack he was steeling himself for never came. Instead, he felt sure hands on his body. He thrashed.

"Relax, relax, I'm not going to hurt you...I mean,

anymore than I just did. I'm really sorry." She sounded genuinely guilty, at least.

David waited until his vision cleared, and found himself staring up at a strikingly beautiful blue-furred jag woman with a vivid scar across her right eye. She looked angry and guilty and worried all at once.

"You hit me," he said, blinking several times.

"You startled me," the woman who had saved his ass at the warehouse replied. "But I'm really sorry. Here, let me look at your head."

He waited while she carefully prodded his head. After a moment, she let out an appreciative sound. "Well, you're not bleeding. You've got a hard head, man."

"So I've been told," David replied. "Can I get up now?"

"Yes," she said, and offered him help up.

He stood, waited for the room to stop tilting and spinning, then looked around. He was in a kitchen. There was a chair nearby, so he went over and sat on it.

"What are you doing here? After that stint at the warehouse I thought you'd be done for the day," she said.

It felt weird chatting with her given that their first two interactions hadn't gone super well. Not that he was ungrateful.

"That was my intent," he replied, "but my situation required another excursion."

She hesitated, then sighed and hopped up on a counter, sitting on it. Her tail poked out to one side, the tip of it laying over the edge, rhythmically thumping against the side of the counter.

"What's your situation?" she asked, almost sounding reluctant.

"You know River View?"

"Yes, and I know it fell last night. You're from there?"

"Yes. Myself and two others are holed up in a cabin. One of them was injured and nearly frozen to death, as we didn't find her until today when we went back to the village. That's why I was in the warehouse: I was looking for medicine. Once I got back, we realized that we were running dangerously low on ammunition.

"So I went to those three buildings at the crossroads back there to search. I found a family living in the garage, also refugees from River View. They have ammo, but lack food and medicine. I found food, now I'm looking for more medicine to give them so that they'll trade the ammo to me," David explained.

The woman looked at him for a long moment with her slit-pupils.

He studied her back.

She was extremely attractive, in a very dangerous kind of way. She had on just a dirty tanktop and some tight shorts and running shoes. Her deep blue fur would grant her a lot of immunity to the cold, and her build, which was lean and wiry, would give her a lot of speed and agility. She had a pistol on one hip, a combat knife on the other, and a backpack slung over her shoulders.

He found it hard not to look at her chest, as her nipples were visible through her tanktop, and she had some nice tits. She was in just fantastic shape.

"My name is Ellie," she said finally.

"David."

"Well, David...to make up for hitting you, I'll show you where there's a little cache of medicine not too far away from here." She hopped up off the counter. "Okay?"

He stood up. "Okay. Thank you."

"Uh-huh. Let's go. I've already searched this place and there's nothing here."

He wanted to search it for himself, and might come back and do so at some point, but he didn't think she was lying to him. So he followed her outside, around to the back of the house, then away from it. They walked for a little while through the forest.

"How do you know about this medicine?" he asked eventually.

"I put it there," Ellie replied.

"Oh. Any particular reason?"

"I might need it in the future," she said.

That made sense. He had the impression that she didn't want to talk, so he tried to keep himself occupied with just searching the area around them. But this place seemed pretty dead.

They kept walking, moving among the dead trees and brittle remains of shrubs and other plant life, little more than corpses now that winter was truly here. Eventually it would warm up again, and everything would resurrect in full bloom. He looked forward to that, to spring, to the showers and the comfortable temperatures.

But from where he stood at this moment, that all seemed like a very long ways off.

Finally, they came to another clearing, where an isolated cabin with a partially collapsed roof resided. They took their time in searching the area, inside and out, to make sure it was secure, and, once it was, Ellie began uncovering her cache, which was apparently hidden behind several pieces of large furniture.

He helped her.

"Are you from around here?" he asked.

"Not originally. I've been here for a little while now."

"Where do you live?"

She frowned fiercely and looked up at him. "Why?"

He felt a bolt of fear shoot through him. "I mean...I'm just curious. Sorry, I guess I can see how that would be a prying question."

She sighed and finished shoving the last piece of furniture out of the way. "I don't really live anywhere, just around the region. I move a lot."

He considered that. "Do you know Cait, by any chance?"

"The redhead? Yeah. She does the same thing. We've worked together a few times. How'd you meet her?"

"Same way I met you."

"She saved your ass, huh?"

David laughed. "Yeah...and then we, uh–"

"What?" she asked, looking at him more intently.

"Uh...spent the night together," he replied awkwardly.

A sly grin crept onto her face. "That sounds like Cait."

She moved to the corner of the cabin obscured by the partially collapsed roof and the furniture they'd just moved, and retrieved a metal case and a small backpack. She came back and set them both on a table, then opened them up and began pulling a few things out of each.

"I'm taking some of this for myself, since it's mine, but I'm leaving the rest with you." She looked at him squarely in the eyes for a second. "You can have some of this, but I want you to give the majority of it to that family."

"Um...okay, yeah, sure. I'll do that," he replied.

"Good." She shoved a few items into her own pack, then pulled it back on. "I'm leaving now. You can find your own way back."

"I...all right, fine. Thank you for your help," he replied.

He wanted to ask her if she'd be more interested in helping him and Evelyn, but obviously she wasn't.

"You're welcome. Bye."

She walked out of the cabin and was gone.

He sighed softly and looked over the supplies. There was a pretty decent haul. Several bottles of antiseptics, two epi-pens, an abundance of different sized bandages and gauze, a ton of painkillers, some injections of morphine, several medical tools, some suture kits, and more.

He took a bottle of painkillers, a bottle of antiseptics, and some gauze, put them in his own pack, then scooped everything else up into the smaller backpack, emptying out the metal carrying case.

That would actually be super useful for holding spare ammunition. It looked solid, lightweight, easy to transport.

Once that was done, he packed up and left.

. . .

"Holy shit...thank you so much," Jim whispered as he looked over the contents of the small pack. "This is going to help a *lot*."

"That was my hope," David replied.

"Okay, um, what do you need?" he asked, zipping up the pack and setting it aside.

They were standing actually inside the garage this time. The door that the man had been guarding led to a front lobby area with a wraparound desk. The windows had been hastily covered with old, oily blankets, and the interior was lit with candles.

Not the safest environment, but it was better than letting zombies see in through the windows, or people.

"We only have weapons that take nine millimeter, so those would be useful, but we could really use a third weapon. Like a shotgun or a rifle? Or an SMG?" he replied.

"We *do* have a spare shotgun," the man said, then sighed. "You earned it."

"Thank you. Could you put whatever you'd be willing to spare in here?" he asked, passing him the container.

"Yes. I'll be right back."

He disappeared through a door at the back of the room, presumably into the garage section. David heard light conversation and waited impatiently, he really wanted to get back to Evelyn. It was going to be dark soon, what with the sun setting so damned early now.

A few minutes later, the man returned, carrying the case and a pump-action shotgun.

"It takes ten gauge shells," he said as he set the weapon down. It came with a shoulder strap, which was nice. "It can hold ten of them."

"Very nice," David replied, looking it over.

It looked to be in pretty good condition.

"There's twenty shells in here, and ten magazines of nine millimeters." He hesitated. "If, uh, you know anyone who would be willing to trade for ammo, we've got more. I mean, anyone you think you could trust. Honestly, the fewer people know we're here, the better. It's...really dangerous out there, nowadays."

"I understand," David said. "I'll keep you in mind. And if my friends and I ever manage to find somewhere safe to live, and there's room, I'll also keep you in mind."

"I would...we'd *really* appreciate that," Jim replied. He offered his hand. "Thank you again. It's so damned hard to find people worth their salt now."

"It sure as hell seems that way," David agreed, shaking it.

He wrapped up the transaction and the conversation, secured the case in his pack and the shotgun over his shoulder after loading it up, thanked the man once more for trusting him and trading honestly with him, and then left.

It was time to go home.

# CHAPTER SEVEN

David wouldn't admit it to anyone else, but he worried himself the whole way home that something had gone wrong.

That he would get there and find the cabin on fire, or Evelyn dead, or the place swarming with monsters or marauders. The problem was that it was possible, even likely, given their current environment.

So it was a deep, deep relief to get home and find it undisturbed. He thought he could faintly hear light conversation, but it stopped immediately as he moved across the floorboards and they creaked with his weight.

That was a good feature of the place, honestly.

He got to the door and opened it up. "It's David, Evie!" he called.

"Thank goodness, come on down," Evelyn replied cheerily.

He moved downstairs and found that the basement looked different.

Mainly it was a lot neater and more organized. There was a little niche of space to the right of the stairs, created by the stairs themselves, and he saw several boxes and other random items pushed up there, looking like Evelyn had shoved them there to get them out of the way. The corner to the left of the fireplace now had a desk and a chair in it, the desktop scattered with paperback novels, some papers, a random collection of pencils and other writing implements, and there was an electric lamp even.

The other corner had the dresser he'd seen earlier, and farther up that wall was a square table with two chairs and a large, solid crate around it.

Their food supplies were stacked on it, as well as a few jugs of water. Finally, there was another desk with a blanket folded neatly and covering the top, as well as a pillow and another blanket, folded even smaller resting at the opposite end of the pillow. He looked at it for a moment, then glanced at Evelyn.

"That's our, uh, infirmary, such as it is," she said.

"Oh," he replied, getting it now. That was why the blanket had been folded so severely, so it wouldn't block the drawers where, no doubt, their medical supplies were stored.

Their sleeping quarters, such as they were, still remained in the center of the room, a big nest of blankets and pillows and clothing that had only been marginally more organized. Sitting on it was the rep woman he'd seen earlier.

"Do you like it?" Evelyn asked.

"Yes, Evelyn. It's fantastic," he replied.

She smiled and he saw she was blushing a little. "I'm glad you like it," she said, then her eyes drifted down to the rep woman and she looked a little embarrassed. "Oh! Um, yes. April, this is David. David, this is April," she said. "She's awake now."

"I can see that. How are you feeling?" he replied as he walked over to the table and set his backpack down on it.

"So much better," she replied. "Thank you so, so much. You both saved my life. Like, legitimately, I would have died there."

"I'm glad I could help. How are your wounds?" he asked.

"They're okay. My biggest problems were dehydration and the cold. I was freezing to death. I'm feeling so much better now, but..." she hesitated, looking suddenly anxious.

"What? What's wrong?" he asked.

"It's okay, April. Just tell him," Evelyn said.

"I...I'm going to be weakened for a few days, so I'm going to be sleeping a lot. And...I'll do it if I have to, but I...it's more dangerous for me to go outside than any other species during the winter, because of my cold-blooded nature, and...please don't kick me out," she whispered.

"April, we're not going to kick you out. We're not like that," David replied.

"I tried to tell her."

"I just...I get so paranoid," she said. "I've always been physically weak, and at a big disadvantage during the winter, and people are so quick to just cut you loose if you're weak..."

"April," David said, and she looked up at him. He was facing her fully now, staring at her intently. "That won't happen here. I promise. Take the time you need to rest up, get back to full strength. You can stay here, and we'll take care of you. All we ask is that you pull your own weight in some way. It doesn't have to be going outside and doing dangerous things.

"It can be simple things: cooking, sorting supplies when we bring it in, I mean hell, even just guarding the place would be fine. As long as you don't betray us, and you're contributing a reasonable amount to the group, it'll be totally fine. And if you feel what we're asking is unreasonable, tell us, and we can all talk about it. I don't want things to be complicated, and I don't want to throw you to the wolves."

"I won't betray you," she said with certainty. "I mean fuck, with just what you've done for me in the past twenty four hours? That's more than anyone has done for me in years. You two are my best friends as far as I'm concerned."

"Well, I'm sure Evie will make you happy, she's amazing. I'll do what I can to be a friend," David replied.

April giggled. "That's what Evie said about you. You two are cute."

"I'm glad you think so," Evelyn replied, grinning broadly. She looked at David. "So what actually happened out there? You were gone for a while..."

He told them both.

He told them about the family at the garage, about Ellie, about the trade. He also brought April up to speed on whatever Evelyn might not have mentioned. As they talked, he sorted out the supplies he'd gathered. They agreed that the case was a good place for spare ammo, and put it on top of the dresser. After that, they got to work making dinner.

Mainly they heated up some of the meat that was in the cans, and once that was done, April slowly pulled herself out of bed (she really wasn't exaggerating about how weak her experience had left her), and they sat around the table and ate. He got to know her as they enjoyed dinner.

"I'm afraid I'm not very impressive," April said. "The only real bargaining chip I have is my medical knowledge. The problem is, I'm not a surgeon or specialist or anything like that, so people mostly think they know at least as much as I do. My true specialty lies in that I know a lot of specific medical facts about how to treat most of the different species. All but the nymphs and the squids, since I've hardly met any. I..." she hesitated.

"What?" Evelyn asked.

"I'm sorry. I've learned not to talk about myself, because whenever I tell the truth, it just gives people red flags and tells them to stay away from me."

"That must be lonely," David said quietly.

She sighed. "It is. I don't have much combat experience. I grew up in a bigger colony on the west coast. A few thousand people lived there. It was good. I lived there for twenty five years. But then the place I was living began to get hit with flooding, and it got really bad. We had to evacuate. We went farther inland.

"After that, it just seemed like we couldn't really find a place to resettle, you know? My friends and family, we all stuck together as much as we could, going from one place to the next. But circumstances began to whittle our numbers down. People would die, people would go missing, people would find a place they really liked and just live there. Me and my family kept getting driven out. People didn't like reps." She shook her head.

"People are assholes," David muttered.

"They sure can be," Evelyn agreed.

"I imagine you must've experienced the same, being a goliath," April said, then her eyes went wide. "Fuck, was that a really mean thing to say? I'm sorry if it was." She let out a half-sigh, half-growl of frustration. "This is why I don't fucking talk to people anymore..."

"No, it's okay, you're right. And I didn't take it as something mean," Evelyn replied. "I actually really do understand. In a way, in my experience at least, goliaths have it pretty bad. I mean, squids and nymphs do, too, but they almost never try to live among settlements. Wraiths have it worst. I've seen people try to kill wraiths. But people get freaked out by our size, and I'm considered short for a goliath. But no, I do get it."

"Okay. So, um, anyway...my mom died two years ago during a fire. And my dad died a year later in a raid. I was an only child, and when he went, I didn't have anyone else," April said.

"I'm so sorry," David replied.

"So am I. I miss them. I...that whole experience strengthened me up a lot. Made me a lot tougher. Which is sad, considering how weak I still am, emotionally and physically. I spent the past year moving from settlement to settlement, just trying to find a place to live, you know? I just wanted to spend time indoors, relatively close to people, with a steady job and a little library to read."

"You like books?" David asked.

"I love them," April replied immediately.

"I'll keep an eye out for them when I'm out."

"Oh, you don't have to do that, but...well, I would really appreciate it. I love reading so much. Probably more than anything else. I can lose a whole day to reading. But you can see why these attributes aren't exactly sought after in a world where most people need to be fast or strong more than they need to be smart."

"I can understand that," David replied. "But we'll appreciate you. Any advice or help you have to give will be useful."

"Thank you," she said, smiling shyly at him. She glanced suddenly at Evelyn.

He'd noticed that the whole time they'd been making and then eating dinner. Something seemed to be bugging her. He yawned suddenly. They'd since finished eating and had sat back from their meals, letting them digest.

He was goddamned exhausted after all the crazy shit he'd had to put up with over the past two days.

"Well, uh, if there's nothing else, I think I'll need to turn in for the night. I'm sure there's a lot more we'll need to be getting to tomorrow," he said.

David looked at April, who stared back at him, then she looked over at Evelyn again, who just smiled at her. "April, go on, ask him the question you wanted to ask him," she said.

David kept looking at April, waiting. She looked at him, and he had the impression that if reps could blush, she would be doing so fiercely.

"So...um...here's the thing. I haven't gotten laid in like a long time. And I was talking with Evelyn about it, and she said she thought you'd be interested in having sex with me, and that you two were in a relationship, but she would be more than okay with you fucking me..."

"Provided I get to watch," Evelyn murmured.

"Yeah. So, um, I mean, if you're not into me, that's fine. I don't want to try and guilt you into it or anything, but...well, I'm *super* tight, if that helps?"

"April, I'm definitely interested," he replied.

"Really?"

"Yes. I think you're very attractive, and I would love to have sex with you."

"Oh thank fucking God," she whispered. "I'm not sex-crazy or anything, but after you haven't had it for a really long time..."

"I definitely understand," David replied as he got to his feet and took off his shirt. "Let me get washed up."

"Okay," she said quietly.

He felt a pulse of excitement go racing through him as he started taking his clothes off. He was glad he'd had that conversation with Evelyn about sex with other women already, and he was honestly surprised he'd already stumbled into an opportunity.

As he finished stripping down naked and then began washing up, using a washcloth, a bar of soap, and a pot of melted snow that Evelyn must have set up for just such an occasion while he'd been out, he found that he was especially looking forward to this encounter.

Not just because it was sex with a new woman, or even an inhuman woman, but because April was a rep. As he'd told Cait earlier, he'd lost his virginity to a rep, and that relationship they'd experienced had always felt special.

And, well, to be completely honest, as a result rep ladies really did it for him. By the time he'd washed off all the accumulated sweat and grime that he'd built up over the course of the day, he saw that April was ready for him.

She was laying on her back in the middle of the blanket nest, nude.

She looked anxious and shy and vulnerable.

He tried to put her at ease as much as he could as he laid down next to her. She had a nice body, though she was very skinny. He doubted she'd been enjoying many real meals lately. Well, ideally that was going to change. She had thin thighs and small, high breasts and smooth, scaly light green skin. He laid down beside her and looked at her.

She looked back at him.

"If you change your mind, let me know, okay?" he asked.

"Okay, I will. I mean, I won't change my mind, but, um, thank you. Trust me, I really want this. I'm just...anxious. I've never been good with getting naked in front of other people. I've always been so skinny and scrawny, you know..."

"I understand," he replied, then reached out and placed a hand on her arm and began to rub it slowly up and down. She shuddered at the contact and her breath caught. "I really do think you're very beautiful, April. I'm very happy to be having sex with you."

She smiled, her eyes closed, like she was focusing intently on his touch. She slowly opened them back up. "Thank you," she whispered. "I'm really happy too. You're...man, you're really hot. I've really got a thing for human guys and you just...you look so good."

He laughed, finding now it was his turn to be awkward. "Uh, thanks," he replied. Then he leaned in and kissed her.

She moaned and kissed him back. They began to touch each other, and it felt wonderful, her hands on his body, shy but eager, growing bolder, and he could feel that she was telling the truth. She really did find him extremely attractive.

And that just felt good. He hoped she was feeling the same thing. There was something truly awful about feeling like you were ugly, and there was something truly wonderful about feeling like you were attractive.

David ran his hands over her smooth, scaly skin, and it instantly brought him back to his awkward, fumbling attempt at lovemaking with his first girlfriend, the one and only chance they had ever had to make love. It had been a lot of things, but mainly it had been good. He kept kissing her, pressing himself against her, and felt her respond in kind.

His hand made a slow glide down her slim body until it found its way to her thighs. She parted them for him, and then she moaned loudly as he ran a fingertip between the lips of her smooth pussy.

"Oh yes," she whispered as they kept kissing. "Please touch me there, David..."

He touched her there, finding her clit and beginning to massage it. She moaned even louder and her hips bucked. She broke the kiss after a few seconds, unable to maintain it, looking off to the side, her face twisting in pure rapture as she squeezed her eyes shut.

"Yes, David, yes, keep–oh fuck–yes, don't stop..." she begged incoherently.

He kept going, kissing her cheek, then along her jaw, then down to her neck. She was panting now, squirming as he pleasured her. David slipped his finger inside of her. April let out a cry of intense pleasure.

"Yes! Oh fuck!" she moaned, her hips jerking as he began to rapidly fuck her with his finger, pushing up hard over and over.

She trembled and shook and before he knew it, she was coming. He felt her vaginal muscles clenching hard around his finger and it got a little wetter, (reps didn't squirt, due to the nature of their bodies, and he was going to need lube), and it was beautiful to watch. Her petite, skinny body squirmed and thrashed and twisted as she cried out in intense pleasure. He kept fingering her through the whole thing.

When she was done, she flopped back, panting.

"Fuck me," she gasped. "Please fuck me."

"Okay, lemme find the lube," David replied.

"I've got you covered," Evelyn said.

He glanced over, slightly startled, as he'd almost forgotten she was there. He tended to get really into it whenever he was having sex. She tossed him a little bottle and he caught it. "Where'd this come from?" he asked.

"I had it on me," she replied.

"Did you now?" he asked as he squeezed some out into his hand.

"Yeah, never know when it might come in handy."

"Well, thank you."

"You're welcome. I'm really enjoying this so far," she murmured, staring intently at the two of them from her seat on the crate. "You two look really good together."

"I'm glad you think so," April said, a little breathlessly.

"It's about to get better," David said as he finished lubing his steel-hard dick up. He tossed the bottle aside and got in between April's legs. Looking down, he saw her tail laying flat between them and that just turned him on more.

Ladies with tails were *hot*.

He laid his cock at the entrance of her slick, scaly pussy and began to work his way in.

"Oh-oh my!" she cried. "That's...oh wow...you're very large..." she whispered. "Careful, now."

"I will be," David replied, and took care to work his way slowly into her pussy.

To help facilitate the process, he reached down and began to rub her clit. She moaned loudly, trembling, and started to pant again. David felt the pleasure begin to rise in him as he got into her pussy.

April. Was. *Tight*. So fucking tight. She definitely on the skinnier end of the spectrum, he could see why she thought he was so big. She was probably a foot shorter than him, maybe a little less, and really thin. It wasn't precisely the same, but it was a little like a goliath dude fucking a human chick. So he just kept easing his way into her pussy.

Eventually, he was comfortably inside, and once that was achieved, he laid down on top of her and began making love to her.

"Oh yes!" she cried, putting her legs up in the air. "Oh my fucking–oh! I'd really forgotten how good this feels! And you're *so* fucking big!" she moaned.

"This *is* even hotter," Evelyn murmured.

David groaned, burying his cock in her over and over again, slipping repeatedly into that insanely tight rep pussy.

She felt different than other women, slicker, smoother on the inside. David took care not to go too hard or fast, because as engaged as she was, he could tell she was definitely still feeling drained and exhausted from her experience. He pushed his way into her again and again and his dick throbbed in response to the hot bliss that was burning into it.

He wanted to come so bad, but he wanted to make her come again first.

As they made out, he reached down between them and began to thumb her clit again. She cried out and her hips jerked. He kept going, screwing her pussy while thumbing her clit, and after about thirty seconds of this she had another screaming orgasm. And it felt so fucking good being in that insanely tight, orgasming pussy that it triggered his own climax.

He cried out, his hips jerking, as he began to come, and his voice joined hers.

The pleasure rolled through him in waves, his whole body twitching in time with his orgasm as he came hard inside of April, filling her pussy up.

He finished coming not long after she did.

When he was finished, he pulled out of her and sat down beside her, getting his breath back. That had been intense. Then he realized something.

"Oh fuck, I'm sorry April, I didn't ask if you cared if I came in you or not," he said.

"It's okay," she replied, "I'm fine with it." She grinned tiredly. "It's hot."

"I agree," he said, feeling relieved.

Evelyn walked over and gave her something to clean herself up with, then fixed him with an intense gaze. "I believe, as your girlfriend, it's my turn," she said.

"That makes sense," he replied. "I'll, uh, need a minute."

"Okay. I have a request."

"What's that?"

She took off her shirt, and he saw she wasn't wearing a bra. Fuck. She had *huge* tits. "I want to be on top," she said.

"I...all right," he replied after a moment.

"Don't worry, I won't let anything happen to you. It'll feel really good."

"I trust you."

Her smile turned from sultry to more sweet, and she took off her pants. "Thank you," she said. "I really appreciate that."

April finished cleaning herself up, then made room for them. "If I fall asleep while you two are fucking, don't take that as an insult, I'm seriously fucking tired."

"It's perfectly okay," Evelyn replied. "We'll try not to go on for too long."

"Given how fucking hot you are and how good your pussy feels, I'm still at that stage in the relationship where you turn me on so much I don't last long," David admitted.

"I kind of like that," Evelyn said as she sat down beside him.

"I'm glad, one of us should."

"Don't worry, I'm sure we'll get to longer screws sooner or later, but honestly fuck sessions that last over half an hour are overrated," Evelyn replied.

"Mmm-hmm," April murmured sleepily. "I really don't have the endurance for it. I like nice, sweet five to ten minute bangs."

"Those are nice," David said.

Evelyn reached out and took his hand, then put it on one of her huge breasts. Man, he really couldn't get over just how fucking big her tits were. They were enormous, immense, gigantic. Bigger than his head. He loved seeing them and touching them.

"Someone's horny again," Evelyn murmured.

Before he could respond, she mounted him, grabbed his cock and slipped it inside of her. He groaned loudly as her slippery, wet pussy accepted his rigid length.

"Oh my fucking God, Evie," he moaned, staring up at her nude body and huge tits and beautiful face.

"I fucking love it when you call me that," she whispered as she began carefully riding his dick.

"It's a really sexy name," he replied, trying to catch his breath.

He'd never actually had sex with another woman so fast after fucking a different woman. Actually, now that he thought about it, this was the most adventurous experience, sexually speaking, he'd been in. He ran his hands up and down Evelyn's tremendous, pale thighs, up to her enormously broad hips, and watched his cock disappear into her inhuman pussy again and again.

"Fuck, I love that dick," she moaned as she began to ride him a little faster.

It was kind of scary having a woman this big riding you, but in a way that just enhanced the encounter, made it even hotter and more erotic.

She kept riding him, just going and going and going, saturating his cock in pleasure and rapturous gratifying bliss, and it was nice to just lay there and be fucked sometimes. After about five minutes she reached down and began to rub her clit, and her voice went up in pitch, her moans becoming faster as she panted.

He loved hearing that so much.

It was like a shot of pure lust, hearing women make those sounds.

She started coming and her vagina clenched around him, muscles spasming, and he felt that hot release of sex juices as she orgasmed.

"Oh fuck, Evelyn!" he groaned as he felt his cock become overloaded with ecstasy.

She made him start coming pretty fast and for the second time that night, he enjoyed the pure, uncut pleasure of orgasming into a completely unprotected pussy. He moaned, losing himself in that bliss, feeling her move against him, the whole thing amplified by the knowledge that there was an attractive, nude woman laying right next to him who he had already fucked.

And then he was finished, and he was spent, and he knew he wasn't getting back up tonight unless there was a genuine emergency.

Evelyn got off him and stood. "Wow, you look dead," she murmured.

"Uh-huh," he managed. "I'm just...it was a long day."

"Yeah, it was," she agreed as she went and began cleaning herself up. "And you just fucked two women. Go to sleep, David, you earned a good rest."

"Thank you, Evelyn," he murmured as he rolled over. April was laying beside him. She was already out. "Evelyn?"

"Yeah?"

"You're an amazing friend, and girlfriend."

She laughed softly. "Thank you, David. You're pretty amazing yourself."

"Goodnight."

"Goodnight."

# CHAPTER EIGHT

The next morning, David woke up a few hours after sunrise feeling very refreshed.

Evelyn was already up by the time he got up, and April was still asleep. In fact, she was still asleep even after he'd washed, dried, dressed, and had breakfast.

"What should happen today?" Evelyn asked after he'd finished his breakfast. They sat at the table together, listening to the fire crackle and April's soft respiration.

"We need to think about water," he said.

"We have ready sources," Evelyn replied.

"Yeah, but we can't count on the snow to stick around forever. There's the river, but we'd obviously need to purify it. Which we can do by boiling it, but...I don't know. Maybe I'm just being paranoid, I guess I want another option."

"Aren't there those tablets?" Evelyn asked. "Purification tablets? You drop them in water and they purify it?"

"Yes," David murmured, thinking about it. "Okay, I guess that's a good thing to look for. Another thing I was thinking about was a map. We don't have any kind of map of the region, and I can't keep all of this in my head at once. I don't suppose you came across anything?" he asked.

"No, no kind of map, but I did get some paper and pencils," she replied, getting up and moving over to the desk. She opened a drawer, rooted around, then returned. "How are you with cartography?" she asked, placing a piece of blank white parchment on the table, then a pencil.

"I can get by," David replied.

He made an X in the middle and wrote *home* next to it. Then he spent a moment, putting down the ruined village, the campgrounds he'd seen, the roads as far as he knew, the garage and restaurant and gas station, the warehouse and watchtower and the few derelict structures he'd come across.

"That watchtower," he said, tapping that X on the map, "I want to go there today and climb it. There might be good supplies in there, but it could also give me a great view of the area, see a few more places to check. We shouldn't count on anyone else for right now. We could be on our own all winter."

"Yeah," Evelyn murmured quietly. "I suppose so."

"But we have each other," he said, and reached out, taking her hand. She smiled and gave his hand a gentle squeeze.

"Yes. We do," she said firmly.

"I'm going to check out the watchtower. I want you to stay here and watch the place, make sure April is okay. Does that sound good?"

"Yes, just please be careful out there," Evelyn replied.

"I will," he said. "I fully intend to come back and enjoy another great night with you."

She smiled and leaned forward and kissed him. He kissed her back for a long, lingering moment, feeling a little thrill of excitement when she used her tongue, then the kiss was over. David got up and began pulling on his cold weather gear.

Once that was in place, he grabbed his pistol and some ammo for it, considered it for a bit, then took the shotgun and some shells. After making sure the guns were loaded and ready to work, he gave Evelyn another kiss and left.

It was time for another day out in cold, miserable hell.

...

David had a pretty decent sense of direction, and as such, he began making his way toward the watchtower in as direct a fashion as he could, straight through the dead forest. That *probably* wouldn't go wrong.

Probably.

Hopefully.

David had decent confidence in himself, but he had certainly found it diminishing, if not outright eroding in the face of all this new horror. The world had always been dangerous for him, but this last year had just been fucking *insane*.

As he walked on, his thoughts drifted to Evelyn, and April. His relationship with them was...very interesting. In the past two days, he had doubled the amount of inhuman sexual partners he'd had in his entire life, which would be more impressive if the number had been higher than two...

Although, you know what? No, fuck that, it was impressive.

David had never really considered himself good looking or charismatic, and counted himself very lucky if he managed to hook up with someone. It didn't happen often, and he didn't see a problem with hiring an escort for the night, although he was often too nervous to try.

But what had happened over the past few days, sexually speaking of course, felt like he'd found a huge cache or won the lottery. (What did that even mean? He heard older people still say it sometimes, but it was one of those phrases he'd never actually learned the meaning behind? What the fuck *was* a lottery? Apparently it was crazy good, but that was all he'd gotten out of it.)

Evelyn was an amazing woman and girlfriend. He'd gotten to know her pretty well over the past week and a half and he was very grateful. Some people you met and just liked, you just connected, and sometimes, if you were really lucky, you sparked.

There were sparks with Evelyn.

Even now it was hard not to go back and spend time around her. She was someone special, and he hadn't had anyone special in his life for years now.

April was a different story.

How he felt about her was...complicated.

On the one hand, he really lusted after her, for a number of reasons. She certainly seemed to like him enough, and that was very appealing. And he also felt very...protective of her. The notion that she was very vulnerable and afraid seemed to call to something in him that he wasn't sure how to respond to. When you put all these things together, it felt a little...exploitative, maybe.

She was obviously relying on him for her own safety, well, him and Evelyn, to be fair.

Because it wasn't like he'd flat out told her 'fuck me or I won't help you'. He'd helped her first, before sex had even become a topic of conversation, and he would gladly keep helping her and protecting her even if she wanted to stop having sex with him. He supposed his only real concern was that if she *did* want to stop having sex with him, she might not tell him. Her personality type made it seem like she'd keep going regardless.

He'd seen people do that before, be dominated by stronger personalities and just do whatever they wanted to do. A lot of people got taken advantage of that way. He'd hate to think of himself doing that to anyone.

Well, so far, things seemed fine.

Although April was still very weak and sleepy, so maybe he'd have a conversation with her about the whole thing after she was back up to full strength in a few days. Did that mean he should stop having sex with her?

He didn't think so...he *hoped* not. She really did seem to want it, and it wasn't like she was intoxicated or anything, just tired.

And fuck, she'd been the one to approach him, not the other way around.

Ultimately, David set the thoughts aside, because he didn't actually feel bad about what was happening, more that he was just paranoid, and he should trust the two women in his life that he was sleeping with to be telling him the truth.

All of these thoughts came to a stop as he heard a soft growl from somewhere nearby.

He raised the shotgun and swiveled left. Something was there. It moved, fast, darted around the trees and began racing towards him. He tracked it with his shotgun, waited, waited...there! He squeezed the trigger. The shell punched it right in the chest and blew a huge hole straight through it, spraying the surrounding area with rotting gore. He made a face as the stench hit him and studied his kill.

It was a stalker, a nymph turned bad.

Fuck but there were a lot of them around.

Were there any real nymphs left in these woods? Or had they all been turned? There was a nasty thought. He made sure it was dead with a pistol shot to the dome and left it after making sure nothing else was lurking around.

There seemed to be an endless supply of undead horrors now. He picked up the pace and hurried on between the trees and skeletal bushes, passing the frozen, unmoving lumps of corpses every now and then.

He saw a deer carcass picked almost totally clean and reminded himself that hunting was back on the table. It wasn't something he enjoyed doing, but he could do it. He knew how to skin and clean and prepare meat, because that was a skill-set you learned if you intended to survive in the wilderness, which most people would have to do at one point or another.

He'd gotten used to living in settlements with nearby farms and canneries, or where other people hunted and sold off the meat. Or, at the very least, he'd traveled in groups where there were better hunters and they'd do it.

He doubted April was great at hunting, but Evelyn might be.

After another few minutes, David stopped, spying something.

Off to the left, maybe fifty feet away: a building. Maybe a house.

He hadn't seen it before. He took a moment to mark it on his map as best he could, then set off towards it. There might be people there, but there might not. It was time to find out. David kept his hand on his pistol as he approached the house. It wasn't very large, just one story, and several of the windows were broken.

It looked pretty abandoned. Which could be the idea. He came into the clearing that the house was built in and scanned the area. Still nothing. He moved up to the front porch, listened, then stepped up to the front door.

There were still no sounds, no hint of movement anywhere nearby.

David opened the door.

Beyond lay a ravaged room with the scattered remnants of furniture, a lot of it broken down to its component parts. There was a door at the back of the room and another to the right. He moved in slowly, gun out now. Going up to the right door, well doorway really, there was no longer a door there, he peered in.

Another room that had probably once been a bedroom. All that remained was a rusty bed frame, complete with springs going every which way. There was a closet, but nothing in the closet. He moved on to the other door.

Here was a lonely, depressing, derelict kitchen. The cabinet doors had all been ripped off, the cabinets themselves cleared out, and a single metal table with a deeply scratched surface was all that remained of anything else. There wasn't even a refrigerator. Just two other doors. One led to a small bathroom, the other to probably another bedroom.

As he hunted around for supplies, David found himself wondering what it was like before all the shit had gone down. By the time he'd been born, the zombie apocalypse had already happened decades ago. Society had already largely reformed, not just around the zombies, but the inhumans, too.

Things were fairly set by then.

Not a lot had changed over the course of his life. From what he had gathered from the older people who had actually been alive when it had gone down, in several ways, not much had changed. Villages and settlements were largely microcosms of the massive cities where millions of people used to live.

The biggest change was currency. Now, people just traded directly. Bullets, food, shelter, their bodies. But back then everything revolved around paper, and electric numbers. He still couldn't quite get the concept of a credit card.

The best way someone had once described the whole thing to him was: *It worked because enough people agreed that it worked.* It still sounded nuts, but less nuts. He supposed he could understand that. Villages worked because enough people agreed not to do certain things, and to punish those that broke the agreements.

But there were just so many concepts that he found extremely difficult to comprehend.

In some ways, he liked this new world better.

Well, the one *before* the sudden rise of new mutations. Everything was...simpler, it seemed. Although a lot more people suffered and died, so that sucked.

In the end, David didn't find anything but bad memories and cold depression lingering in that house, and he left it quickly, almost as though he could feel the lingering ghostly remains of whoever had once owned it before the apocalypse.

And as he stepped back outside, he was unhappy to feel a cold, strong gust of wind blow across him. He looked up. It was darker, and grayer.

There was very likely a storm brewing.

How long until it hit? How bad was it to be?

Hard, if not impossible, to tell, but if he had to guess, he'd say that maybe he could get to the watchtower, search it, and go home. Maybe. He stood there, considering what to do, tempted to just turn around and go home. But now was the time to be bold, he supposed.

There was very little in the way of a safety net, and the food they had wouldn't last. Not with Evelyn's intake, and he absolutely hated the thought of her going hungry simply because she was a goliath. No, he was going to go find some more supplies.

David set off once more.

...

By the time he finally found the watchtower, it was starting to snow.

It was still light, but it wasn't a good sign. And then everything changed as he heard gunshots and someone shouting angrily nearby. The voice was familiar. David pulled out his pistol and ran off, towards the sounds of the shots.

He saw muzzle flare and several moving shapes.

And a familiar blue-furred figure.

"Ellie!" he screamed, and popped off a shot at one of the shapes, what he recognized as even more of the awful, sleek stalkers. The shot was good, punching it in the back of the head and blowing its brains out. "I'm here to help!"

"David?! What the fuck!? Whatever! Help!" she yelled in response.

There were still a dozen of them.

He opened fire into the thickest knot of them, half a dozen clustered together and moving in on Ellie. Emptying the magazine into them, he managed to put down four. Then he holstered his pistol and snatched up his shotgun in one smooth move.

Two were coming after him now. He aimed and

fired, blowing one's head clean off its shoulders. The other strafed and came for him, shrieking madly, claws out as it prepared to rip his guts out.

He put a shell through its neck and sent its head flying in one direction, body collapsing in the other. After that, David helped Ellie clean up the survivors, emptying his shotgun in the process. They also had to put down a few zombies that showed up looking for trouble.

Once they had both quickly reloaded their weapons, they took a moment to search the zombie corpses. They both worked in silence, the snow falling all around them. David managed to get his hands on a half-dead book of matches and some nuts and bolts.

If Ellie got anything, she didn't make mention of it.

"Thank you," she said begrudgingly as they finished their search and stood up.

"You're welcome," he replied, trying not to take offense. Ellie seemed like the kind of woman who hated relying on anyone for anything, and helping her out was almost like an insult.

"What are you doing here?" she asked.

"Scouting the area for supplies," he replied. "I was going to get up into that watchtower, try to sketch a map of the area, and find some purification tablets. And anything else."

"Why purification tablets?" she asked.

"I'm paranoid. I want to have my bases covered."

"Hmm. A sound strategy." She hesitated, her tail flicking behind her. She looked around, then slowly looked back at him. "Come up in the watchtower with me. I may be able to help you, and we may need to wait out the storm there."

"All right."

He followed her to the watchtower, which looked weathered but stable, and they walked up the ramps that wrapped around its base. When they got to the top, they had to be a good forty feet up off of the ground, and the view was just spectacular.

He could see trees, so many trees. Even with the snowfall limiting visibility the view was impressive. After admiring it for a bit, he walked into the room at the top of the tower with Ellie and looked around. Clearly, this was a space someone had set up for themselves.

"Is this your place?" he asked.

"In a manner of speaking," she replied. "I share it with a few others. Like Cait. It's a little like an emergency location."

"Oh," he said, a little disappointed. So he wouldn't be able to raid it.

"Listen..." Ellie said, sounding vaguely reluctant, "I'll let you in on a little secret, since you seem on the level. I actually ran into Cait since last we spoke and she spoke fondly of you. So if you come across a place like this, and you see a sign like this," she pointed to the door frame, where he saw a circle with an X carved through it, "then it belongs to us. Myself and Cait and a few others. We all have an understanding. You can take some supplies if you need them, but you're expected to leave something in return. And if you're in surplus and can spare it, it would be appreciated if you could stock something extra."

"Oh...that sounds fair," he replied. "All right, let me see what I've got, because we could use some food. Right now, that's our biggest need."

"You said you were trying to map out the area,

did you mean that literally?" she asked.

He set down his backpack. "Yeah. Why?"

"Let me see what you have so far. I might be able to help," she said.

"Okay, that would be really appreciated."

He gave her the map and the pencil, then decided on what to pull out. Finally, he settled on a flick-knife, a little bottle of painkillers, and the matches he'd found. He then took a look around the area. Everything was packed in around the edges of the room in a tight, tidy fashion.

There was a bed, a cast-iron stove with a vent up to the ceiling, a pair of desks with chairs, what looked like a work area meant for basic repairs, a neatly made cot, and finally a set of shelves. He poked around until he found a stash of food.

After some deliberation, he took four cans of chopped beef and put his own supplies in another drawer.

"Could you get the fire going?" Ellie asked. She was drawing on his map.

"Sure," he replied, and set to that task after putting away the food in his pack.

There was a stack of neatly cut firewood beside the stove, and he put a log in on top of the remains of the previous fire and got a new one going. After he finished with that, a comfortable warmth began to fill the room. He looked out. At one point, all four walls had had windows, but that had obviously changed.

One side was completely boarded up, that was the one that held the bed. There were patchwork jobs plugging up a few of the others, some with sheet metal, the rest with wood. The other windows were dirty but looked to be intact.

He sat down on the bed, looking out the nearest

window at the worsening storm. The winds shrieked madly now and snow blew hard. The watchtower creaked, but Ellie didn't seem worried. She worked without pause for half an hour.

Finally, she stood up. "There, I have done what I could."

"Thank you, I really appreciate it," he said as he joined her at the desk.

The map was a lot more filled in, although much of it was still blank. She'd gone so far as to add in a few more roads, the perimeter of the forest, the river, and several more structures. He had the idea that she actually knew much more, but was reluctant to give up that information. Well, this was more than he could have hoped for, honestly, so he was glad.

For another half hour neither of them spoke.

He kept wanting to make conversation, but Ellie's body language made it clear she didn't want to talk. So he sat on the bed and watched the storm, mostly. It was too dangerous to go out, now. Too easy to get lost, or get grabbed by something that had much better senses and could track you easily, blizzard or no. Ellie moved restlessly about the room, checking drawers and items, never staying in one place for too long.

Her tail was twitching with increased agitation.

Finally, she spoke to him.

"I think we may have to wait out the storm here for some time," she said.

"I'm okay with that. Evelyn and April will be worried, but there's not much I can do about that," he replied.

Ellie stood at one of the windows, staring out it. "So you were at the village when it went down?" she asked.

"Yeah."

"What was it like?"

"About what you'd expect. I was sleeping when it happened. Woke up to a bunch of assholes raiding the place, lighting things on fire, and that drew in a shitload of monsters and Evelyn saved my ass, and we ran until we found some abandoned cabin," he replied.

Another pause. "Who are they, to you? The two women you're staying with."

"Well, I met Evelyn about a week and a half ago on the road into the region. We became very fast friends and now we're together. And April, well, we rescued her from the village yesterday...fuck, was it just yesterday? Feels like a week. Anyway, we're getting to know her. She seems really nice and we, um...we got close pretty fast," he said, feeling heat creep up his neck onto his cheeks.

Ellie turned around suddenly. "You're fucking both of them?"

"Wow, that's...a personal question," he muttered.

"Then tell me to fuck off and it's none of my business if you don't want to answer."

"No, it's just...yeah. I'm fucking both of them. Evelyn said she doesn't mind and April was really lonely and *really* likes me apparently, and I think she's pretty and...man, this is really personal," he said, laughing nervously.

Ellie shrugged. "Impersonal conversations are boring."

"Says the woman who has outright refused to tell me basically anything at all about herself beyond her first name and might as well be wearing a sign that says 'fuck off,'" he replied, reasonably enough, he felt.

She glared at him, then sighed. "Fine, that's a fair point. I don't trust easily, David. That shouldn't surprise you, unless you're a lot stupider or a lot more sheltered than you look."

"No, I, uh...I get it," he replied. "I understand. I'm not trying to be a jerk or anything."

"Why are you so *nice?*" she asked suddenly. "No one is nice anymore without a motive, what the fuck's your motive?"

"What?" he replied, startled. "I mean...staying alive? Helping people?"

"Really?" she asked, stepping closer, almost challenging him. "Your motive is to help people?"

"Yes," he said, feeling suddenly defensive, and a little angry. "You think I'm a piece of shit or something? Do you think I fuck people over? I gave that family the food, you know. I did exactly what I said I would."

She pursed her lips, then looked away. "I'm sorry, that was mean. I'm...you make me suspicious, because my instincts tell me to trust you."

"Why is that so bad? Do you have shitty instincts or something?"

"No! I just...I have been fucked over before by people I thought I could trust, okay? I don't even know why I'm having this conversation."

With that, she suddenly turned around and walked back over to one of the desks. She sat down heavily and stared out the window.

David sighed softly. He watched the wind continue to toss the snowflakes around.

It was going to be a long day.

...

Three hours passed.

It was a grueling three hours, because Ellie seemed intent on being stubbornly frustrated and silent. He wasn't sure if he'd done something to piss her off, but he didn't want to make it worse. He thought that it really was as simple as she'd presented it: her instincts told her to trust him, and that made her suspicious.

Man, that had to fucking suck.

He passed the time as best he could.

First he worked on his pistol, taking it apart and cleaning as best he could manage, then reassembling it. After that he performed another search of the watchtower, in case there was anything he missed that might be really useful, since he'd only actually taken four cans of food. And he actually found something.

It wasn't terribly useful to him in a survival sense, but he thought it could have a lot of value to April. It was a battered old paperback that still looked like it served its basic purpose. It was some kind of fantasy novel, with a big bulky shirtless guy on the cover holding a huge sword, and some dragons and mountains in the background. He wondered if April liked fantasy stories.

"Can I have this?" he asked.

Ellie looked back over her shoulder, her expression frustrated, like she was gearing up to be angry, but then she saw the book and just looked confused.

"It's for April, she really likes books," David explained. "And I wanted to do something nice for her, after all she's been through."

Ellie sighed and turned back around. "Yes, take it."

"Thank you."

She grunted a response. He slipped the book into his backpack and went on trying to find ways to kill time.

Still the storm raged, showing no signs of slowing down.

At some point, he broke out dinner, though all it was was a can of peaches.

He had more, and he wanted to eat more, but he needed to save what food he had. When the food was gone, he eventually pulled back out the novel he'd salvaged and decided to try and read it. Although at first he wasn't certain about it, by the second chapter he found himself very interested.

And before he knew it, he'd gone through most of the book and when he looked up, it was black outside. Still, the snow blew, the winds howled, and Ellie sat at the desk. He'd been aware that she'd been doing things while he'd been reading.

At one point she'd been exercising, and that had been distracting, because she still wasn't wearing a whole lot and she looked really good.

And then Ellie let out a heavy sigh suddenly. "I guess we're spending the night here," she said.

"I guess so," he replied. "Is that...a problem?"

"No," she said, and stood up suddenly. She turned to look at him, and her tail was lashing more and more. "I have an offer."

"Oh...kay," he replied. "What is it?"

"I'm willing to have sex with you, if you're interested."

David stared at her. She stared back.

Ellie was a very strange woman. And that's exactly what he told her.

"So you're saying no to having sex with me?" she asked, shifting subtly so that her body, already showcased fairly well in her tight, thin clothes, stood out even more.

"That's not what I'm saying," he replied quickly. "I'm just saying–"

"That you think I'm weird. I get it. Look, David, I'm tired. I'm not interested in explaining to you why I am the way I am. I'm interested in sex, and you're pretty cute, and you seem on the level, and we're stuck here anyway. So, yes?"

"Yes," he replied quickly.

"Good." She took off her top and dropped it on the floor, freeing her beautiful, firm breasts. They were of a decent size, kind of big on her lean frame. "Then take off your clothes and get in that bed, David."

"Yes, ma'am," he replied, and stood up.

She smirked smugly as she started to take her boots off.

Both of them stripped, David disrobing very eagerly.

Evelyn *had* given him a free pass to sleep with other women, so...yeah, he was going to do this. Ellie was *amazingly* hot. Even if she was kind of cold and a little strange and very intimidating, she was hot. Actually, that last one just made her hotter.

David thought that maybe somewhere along the line, some wires had gotten crossed in his head, because intimidating women just turned him on.

They slipped into bed, and he immediately knew that Ellie was fantastically fit and dexterous. Everything she did had an immense, competent ease to it. She got on top of him suddenly as they settled beneath the blankets of the bed and pushed him down, staring at him with her wide slit-pupil cat eyes. She was vibrantly beautiful and the expression on her face changed her appearance a lot.

She looked...happy, actually.

He thought it was the first time he'd seen her enjoying herself.

She leaned in and kissed him, deeply and passionately, slipping her rough tongue into his mouth, and he groaned and kissed her back, feeling her rub her soft, warm, furry body against his own. He could feel her tight, toned muscles beneath her fur.

Her breasts pushing against his chest. He got a hand between them and groped one of them, groaning again at how good and firm it felt. His other hand sought the smooth curve of her ass, and he found it, gripping it, then caressing it. She moaned into the kiss, continuing to twist her tongue with his.

After a moment, he slipped his hand up to her tail and loosely gripped it.

She gasped, breaking the kiss.

"Oh, I'm sorry, should I not have?" he asked, letting go.

"I..." she looked uncertain, indecisive for the first time since they'd met, chewing on her lower lip, then she slowly smiled. "You can touch it."

"Thank you," he said, and again gently gripped her tail.

She shuddered and moaned, then resumed kissing him.

Ellie felt wonderful. Her firm, toned body, her soft, warm fur, the way she was moving against him. David was given the impression that she was a very lively lover. And he was going to find out very soon.

In fact, after another moment, she suddenly shifted, gripped his cock, and slipped it inside of herself, then slid her very tight pussy down his rigid length.

"Oh *fuuuuck...*" he moaned.

"Mmm...you like jag pussy, don't you?" she murmured, staring down at him.

"Yes..." he groaned, gripping her firm hips. "Oh my fucking God I do."

"You've been fucking that goliath and rep pussy, it's time to show you how good jag vagina is," she said, and began to ride him furiously.

"Oh fuck, Ellie!" he cried as the pleasure slammed into him like a hammer.

"That's fucking right," she growled, gripping his shoulders tighter, bearing her teeth at him as she bounced on his dick, shoving it hard up into herself, fucking her pussy with it like crazy, "you fucking *love that pussy!*"

"Yes!" he cried, and thrust up into her, unable to keep from doing so. "Yes! I love it! *Fuck, I love it, Ellie!*"

He was completely lost in the sex there for a bit.

He didn't know how long they fucked, only that it seemed to go on for a long time, with him staring up at her perfect, firm, bouncing tits and at her face, caught in a mask-like appearance of determined lust. At some point he realized that she had her claws out and was digging them into his skin, and it hurt, but he was too into fucking her to care.

The sounds of their voices screaming and grunting and half-formed incoherent words filled the watchtower as the storm shrieked madly around them.

She came three times, and the third time, he couldn't hold back any longer.

"I'm gonna...fucking...go!" he warned her.

"Do it. Fucking come in me," she growled. "Fucking do it, David. Now! *Now!*"

"*OH FUCK ELLIE!*" he screamed and he came in her.

He came *so* much inside of her, and he could feel her stirring his cock around inside of her orgasming pussy, magnifying the pleasure to almost painful levels, but he was completely lost in her, in their furious fucking.

He emptied himself into her, pumping her jag pussy full of his human seed, and carried on for what felt like a long time. When he was finished, he blinked several times, feeling as though he was teetering on the edge of exhaustion, of passing out, and she was still on him, staring down at him, a look of immense satisfaction on her beautiful, dangerous face.

"Sleep," she said, and got off of him.

He began to say something, and then he fell asleep.

# CHAPTER NINE

"David...what are you doing?"

"Mmm...I was having a dream...fuck, I'm so horny..."

"Ugh, you boys and your horny dicks, here...hold on..."

He was shifting around, barely awake, but being driven nearly mad with lust and intense, powerful sexual desire. She pulled him on top of her, and spread her legs, and the second he had willing access from her, he slipped his cock into her pussy and moaned very loudly. It was pitch black out, only a faint orange glow coming from, he realized, the stove with the fire to keep them warm.

Well, to *help* keep them warm.

They were keeping each other warm right now.

"Oh *yes,* David..." she moaned as he began hammering away at her pussy.

He couldn't help himself, driving into her again and again, his hips working of their own accord as he buried his entire length into her.

"Fuck, you feel big..." she whispered, her hands on his back, and then her legs wrapping around him. "God yes, fuck that pussy," she moaned.

"Oh my fucking...oh Ellie, you feel so good..."

"You're very lucky I let you do this, David," she murmured in his ear.

"Yes...yes I am..." he moaned. "Oh my fucking...oh fuck!" he gasped, and he started to come inside of her. She held him in the very dim glow of the fire, held him as he came inside of her, as he orgasmed against and within her.

And then he was finished, and he carefully pulled

out of her and fell onto his side.

"Thank you, Ellie..." he whispered, then yawned.

"Go back to sleep," she said, and kissed him.

And then he was asleep again.

...

David woke up to someone touching his dick.

"Come on...don't play like you're asleep..."

"What the fuck...what's going on?" he muttered, rubbing at his eye, trying to figure out where the fuck he was and what the hell was going on.

He fully opened them and saw Ellie, naked and amazingly fit, sitting next to him. She was staring at him intently.

"I'm horny," she said simply.

He looked up at her. "Get on your hands and knees."

"Oh, you got it," she replied eagerly, and he got up to make room for her.

He was pretty goddamned turned on himself. For the moment, there was nothing but him and her and getting to fuck the shit out of her. David got onto his knees behind her as soon as she was in place, slipped his cock into her vagina, grabbed her hips, and started fucking her. Her pussy was *so* wet! Evelyn had a really wet pussy, but he thought Ellie's was wetter. Certainly she was tight as well, and just really *hot*.

She had an amazing pussy.

It reminded him of the jag prostitute he'd fucked a while back. Her pussy had been amazing too. He groaned, gripping her hips tightly and staring down at her toned ass as he slammed into her again and again.

Ellie hung her head, moaning loudly as she took his cock.

Like most morning sessions he'd enjoyed, this one didn't last long. It was a quick fuck. He made sure she got off before he did, reaching up under her, finding her clit, and rubbing it vigorously. It was very satisfying to hear her screaming her head off, especially when it went up in intensity as she began to orgasm.

And he fucking pounded the fuck out of her climaxing pussy.

He came into her a third time, pumping her full of his seed, then he pulled out of her and sat down on the side of the narrow bed, trying to finish waking up. That fuck session sure helped. She fell forward onto the bed, breathing heavily.

"*That* is the way to wake up," she muttered.

He murmured an agreement, then got up and moved over to his pack. Crouching down, he pulled out a bottle of water and a washrag, then went about the process of cleaning up. He'd accumulated a lot of sweat and grime, especially from the *three* fuck sessions he'd had with Ellie.

Goddamn, that woman could *fuck*.

David winced suddenly as his shoulders hurt and he looked at one of them. There was blood, dried blood, and four puncture wounds.

"What the hell..." he muttered.

"What? Oh..." Ellie laughed sheepishly. "Uh...sorry about that," she said. He looked back at her. It was weird seeing her look bashful, especially with her being naked. "When I get really into it, you know, it's hard to control..."

"I'll take it as a compliment," he replied, and carefully washed the wounds.

"I'm glad," Ellie said. She seemed uncomfortable, and he couldn't blame her. Given how tough she was, how hard it was for her to trust...well, it would probably be difficult to confront the fact that she'd just done something that would take a *lot* of trust. And she probably wasn't really ready to examine the full ramifications of that.

Well, he had no intention of making it difficult for her.

She'd made herself vulnerable to him, and he appreciated that. Neither said anything as she cleaned herself up as well, and then they both dressed. He looked out the window as she offered to get breakfast ready from the watchtower's own supply. It was done snowing, and it had dumped probably a good dozen inches on them last night.

Great. He wasn't looking forward to trekking back home through that.

Breakfast was a quick but good meal of bacon and bread that was only a little stale. They ate quickly, both of them eager to get places. He wanted to go home, to see Evelyn and April again, and make sure they were okay.

"Ellie," he said as they were pulling their backpacks on.

"Yeah?" she asked hesitantly.

"Thank you...for everything. For saving me, and sharing with me, and...fucking me. It was absolutely incredible."

"Tell me something, was it better than your other girlfriends?" she asked.

"I...don't want to answer," he replied.

She smirked. "I was better. Don't worry, I'll keep your little secret. You weren't all too bad yourself, David." She hesitated, glanced out the window. "Look, maybe I'll swing by this cabin of yours and meet the others. See if there's anything I can offer for help."

"We would *really* appreciate that," he said. "Oh yeah, I just remembered...do you know where there's any purification tablets?"

She frowned, studying him again with that slightly calculating, slightly paranoid look. "If you go due north, you'll run into a sheer rock wall. There's a cave in it. Go to the back of the cave, behind a big boulder, and shoved in the back of a little niche there is a box. You'll need a light to find it properly. There's supplies in there. They're mine. There's purification tablets in there. You can have them, but don't take anything else. Only the tablets."

"I understand. Thank you," he replied.

"You're welcome." She stared at him again, her gaze suddenly almost...beseeching, like she wanted to ask him something, or say something, but then the look passed and the calm flatness returned. "Good luck."

"You too."

They left the watchtower and parted ways.

. . .

It was a pleasantly easy task to find the tablets.

David left the tower and struck out due north.

He didn't run into anything as he tracked down first the cliff sheer, and then the cave. And it was pretty easy to find. The cave was decently lit, for being a cave, due to the way the sunlight fell. He tracked down the little niche at the back and, using his lighter for the final portion of the hunt, he indeed found the cache she'd indicated. There was a metal box that he had to pull out and unlatch before opening up.

It was packed with supplies: some food, some bullets, some medical supplies.

He found the tablets and pocketed them, then left the rest where it was, resealed the box, and hid it back as best he could. As he started making his way back home, he spied one of the other structures in the area that Ellie had marked on his map.

Although he was tempted to make a short detour, he didn't, because he *really* wanted to get home and see Evelyn and April. And he imagined they were probably pretty fucking worried about him by now. So he passed it by and kept on walking, making a beeline for the cabin they now called home.

Twenty minutes later, he was there.

Before he even got to the front door, it was yanked open. For a second, he felt pure fear, as he thought something was coming out to get him. Then he relaxed as he saw Evelyn duck down and hurry out. She was coming to get him all right, just not in a bad way.

"David!" she cried.

"Hello, Evel–oof!" he replied as she swept him up in a hug that literally took his feet off the ground. "Are you okay?"

"I'm fine," she replied, "*now* I'm fine. What happened?"

He kissed her and, after a moment, she let him down. "I found Ellie and saved *her* this time. We were near that watchtower I mentioned when the storm came in, and we ended up getting kind of stranded there..."

Evelyn slowly stopped looking worried, but suddenly she smiled. David was unhappy to realize he was blushing. A *lot*, it felt like.

"You fucked her, didn't you, you bad boy?" she

asked.

"I...three times," he admitted.

"Wow," said a new voice.

David looked around in surprise, and then looked past Evelyn. April was standing in the doorway with a blanket wrapped around her.

"Hi, April," he said.

"Hello, David," she replied with a small, shy smile. "I'm glad you're home safe."

"Me too."

"So you fucked Ellie three times, huh? Wow. She must have been a stellar fuck."

"Oh she *was*...uh, anyway. I got the tablets. And some more food. Not a lot, though. That's why I want to go back out today."

"You aren't going *anywhere* until I get some sex," Evelyn said.

"Uh...wow, okay." He looked back up at her. "So you're...okay that I fucked Ellie?"

"Of course. I'm not lying, David. I don't care that you fucked her. Just...come back home to me and fuck *me* and do nice, fun things with me. I don't care that there's a list, so long as I'm at the top of it. I think that's fair," she replied.

He reached out and took her hand. "I do, too. And you're amazing, and you will always be my number one, Evelyn."

"You two are really cute," April said. They looked back at her, then started walking back towards the cabin. "Can I have sex, too?" she asked as she made room for them. "I kind of, um...I'm remembering how good it felt, and how much I love having it with a guy I can really trust and like and am super attracted to, and you are all of those things, David, and...I really want more dick."

"I will be happy to fuck both of you," he replied.

"No surprise there," Evelyn murmured.

"Quiet," David said, and he smacked her enormous ass.

"You're a very bad boy," she said. "Now fuck me."

"Let's go," he replied, and went towards the basement.

They made their way down the stairs. David felt his heart begin to hammer harder in excitement. This was going to be awesome. Apparently Evelyn and April were comfortable enough to be fucked at the same time. Well, they *had* seen each other getting screwed already. This was shaping up to be a *really* nice relationship.

Once they were all downstairs, they began to strip.

David watched the two women as they got naked. Evelyn's huge boobs looked amazing as they came out, though he noticed April was still a little shy. Especially when she noticed that he was watching her.

"What?" she murmured.

"I just...like seeing women get undressed," he replied.

"Who doesn't?" Evelyn asked.

"Sorry if I'm making you uncomfortable," he said.

"No, it's fine. It's just, you know, something I've always had trouble with." She took off the dress that she was wearing after dropping the blanket. And she didn't have anything on underneath the dress, it turned out.

"You are *really* hot," he murmured as he got out of his boots.

"Thanks," she murmured, rubbing one arm slowly, looking at him demurely.

"You really are," Evelyn said. "You're a very beautiful woman, April."

"Thank you, Evelyn. And you're just...unbelievable," April replied as she stared at her. Evelyn finished getting naked by taking off her panties.

"Really?"

"Oh yes. You're just...so...*big*. And *beautiful*. You're *so* beautiful. I read a lot of romance books, and sometimes they gush about how divine and angelic and just stunningly beautiful the leading ladies are, and you're like that. You're amazing."

"Yes you are," David agreed.

Now Evelyn was blushing fiercely. "Well...thanks." She laughed nervously.

"Let's do this," David said.

They all laid down on the mess of blankets and pillows and clothes they called a bed, and David immediately began kissing and groping Evelyn.

April laid on her other side, and took to licking one of her pink nipples, making her moan into the kiss. He laid his hand on her other enormous breast and groped and squeezed it, wholly unable to even begin to get it in his grasp. She had gratuitously huge tits and some part of him just really liked that. He loved kissing her more, feeling her tongue in his mouth, her body against his, all her hot, soft skin.

He made out with her for a while, and then he moved over to April, giving her some attention. He didn't want her to feel left out. They made out as he ran his hands over her smooth, scaly body, groping her small, high breasts and her trim, tight thighs, and then her tail. Her tail was very sexy. And then he slipped a finger inside of her, and she cried out, bucking her hips.

"Oh my!" she cried.

"You like that?" he replied.

"Y-yes...fuck..." she moaned, and kept making out with him passionately as he fingered her, rapidly sliding his finger in and out of her tight opening.

He did it until she had an orgasm, and wow, did April look sexy coming. She twitched and writhed and moaned, clenching and releasing her fists over and over again, and her tail jerked several times. When she was finished, he pulled back and let her rest.

"Evie, spread your legs," he said, and began moving.

"Okay," she replied, sounding eager. He shifted and then got in between her enormous thighs. "Oh! You're going to–okay, wow."

He rested so that he was facing her crotch, then settled in to pleasure her. He began licking her clit, and as soon as he did, she shivered hard and let out a cry. "Oh wow! That's–oh my! Yes! Oh fuck, it's been *way* too long..." she moaned.

"Wow, this is really hot," April whispered.

"Yes–ah!–it is!"

David kept going, thoroughly enjoying pleasuring her. There were levels to it. He liked pleasuring women in general, and he especially liked pleasuring his girlfriend. He wanted to make her feel good. But there was a whole other level to it now. Something about pleasuring a goliath who was over a foot taller than he was was just fucking awesome.

He licked her clit over and over again, tonguing it and caressing it, massaging it, and feeling her whole body writhe and twist around him. And the *noises* she was making…

Evelyn was crying out and muttering incoherently, spreading her legs out, begging for more. And he happily gave her more. David continued eating her out until she let out a loud squeal of pleasure and began to orgasm. He had slipped a finger into her by this point and he began furiously fucking her with it as she came.

*"OH MY FUCKING GOD DAVID YES! OH FUCKING SHIT FUCKING YES! YES! YES! HOLY FUCK! YESYESYESYESYESYES!!!"* she screamed wildly.

Honestly, he was surprised he didn't get somehow hurt during the orgasm.

When she was finished, Evelyn went slack against the blankets and let out her breath in a very long sigh. "Oh my God...thank you so much, David. That was...whew! That was the best orgasm I've had in some time. You are a *very* good boyfriend."

"Well, you're a pretty good girlfriend so far," he replied, and she laughed. He looked over at April as he propped himself up. "Your turn."

"Oh my. I, um...thank you," she murmured.

"You're welcome," he replied, and shifted over until he was between her legs. He looked down at her tail, which was laying flat between her legs, and ran a finger up it. She let out a startled sound and shivered violently.

"Sensitive?" he asked.

"Yes...very. Oh wow," she whispered.

He grinned, then leaned in and went to work on her. She moaned loudly as he parted the taut, smooth lips of her rep vagina and began to lick at her flat, pale green clit. He saw her thigh muscles bunching and rippling beneath her skin as she tried to control herself.

"Oh yes! I actually haven't–ah! Oh my fucking...oh!–haven't been–mmm!–eaten out in over a year...oh yes, David!"

"You must be in heaven right now," Evelyn murmured.

"Yes! I am! Oh your tongue is just–oh! OH FUCK!" she shrieked, and then she was enjoying another beautiful, full-bodied orgasm. He kept licking throughout her climax, feeling her move and shift against him, her tail twitching back and forth against his chest, listening to the amazing sounds she was making.

When she was finished, she gasped, "Fuck me, David!"

"I can do that," he replied.

He took a moment to clean up and rub his cock down with lube, then he got on top of her and began working his way into her pussy. She moaned extremely loudly, her whole body nearly convulsing in pleasure as he penetrated her. April reached up and grabbed him as he began making love with her, slipping his cock deeper and deeper into her inhuman pussy.

She wrapped her legs around him, pulled him down against her, and kissed him deeply.

"You are *amazing,*" she gasped between kisses.

He wasn't sure how to reply to that, so he just kept kissing her and fucking her, pushing his cock into her again and again, eliciting loud cries of pleasure from her. She pushed her hips against his own, forcing his cock deeper and deeper into herself. They kept this up for about a minute and a half before she demanded they change positions.

"How do you want to be?" he asked.

"On top," she said. "I want to make you fucking come so hard."

"Oh, all right," he replied, then he grabbed her and rolled himself. She let out a little cry of surprise as she ended up on top of him.

"You're strong," she whispered.

"You're small," he replied.

"You're both right," Evelyn murmured, watching him.

He groaned as she began to furiously ride his cock, fucking herself with it and nearly overwhelming him with pleasure. It felt amazing. After barely another minute he could tell he was going to pop.

David didn't want to, he wanted to last longer, but April was *tight*! Like, *really* fucking tight as hell! And she was just going and going and *going*...

"April..." he groaned, panting. "You gotta stop or I'm gonna come in you..."

"That's exactly what I want," she growled, and began going faster.

"Oh fucking–fuck! April!" he cried, and then he was gone, coming hard inside of her.

She looked uncharacteristically satisfied and sure as he pumped her full of his seed, his cock jerking violently inside of her, spraying it all out in hard spurts. She moaned, staring down at him, taking his hands in hers and holding them, lacing their fingers together. He felt intimately connected to her as she locked eyes with him, holding his gaze with her own, pleasuring him with her body, letting him come inside of her bare pussy.

Pleasure washed through his body, a cocktail of bliss and rapture and pure perfect ecstasy.

He came inside of her for what felt like a long time, his cock throbbing madly in response to the tremendous pleasure she was giving him. When he was finished, he fell back, going slack, panting. She smiled down at him.

"You look pretty self satisfied," he said as he got his breath back.

"It's...been a long time since I've realized I could make a guy come, you know? Since I've felt in control of a sexual situation. It's a really good feeling to be having sex with someone who just...likes you, you know? You aren't having sex with me for any other reason than you want to. You aren't trying to get something out of me, you aren't giving me a pity fuck, you just really like me, and I just really like you. And that kind of sex is just amazing."

"It is," he agreed. "It really is. Whew..." he let out his breath in a long exhalation.

"When will it be my turn?" Evelyn asked.

"Very soon. I just...I need a minute," he replied.

"After that, I don't blame you." She reached out and ran a hand across his chest. He reached up and took it, brought it close to his face and kissed her warm, smooth skin.

"I love how affectionate you are," she murmured.

"Me too," April said, and got up off him, making him groan as his cock fell out of her.

He held Evelyn's hand and waited for his energy to come back.

...

"So, maybe we should talk about our plans," David said as he sat down at the dinner table.

"Like how?" April asked.

"I guess, for the winter."

"Well..." She looked around the basement they

called home. "This place is livable."

David frowned, considering it. He looked at Evelyn.

"I...suppose it might do," she murmured uncertainly.

"I was thinking of something a bit more ambitious, and sustainable. Evelyn and I found some campgrounds not too long ago, and I paid them a visit earlier. They're in pretty good condition, from what I can tell. They're kind of cleared out, but there's a good dozen solid buildings with an actual, real perimeter, a fence. It'll take some work, to be sure, but there will be room to grow, and I think it would be a lot safer than this. Plus, if we find other people, we could actually afford to have some space for them to live."

"Other people?" April asked uncertainly.

"I mean, a lot of people were displaced when that village half burned to the ground. I don't know, it's just a thought. But this place isn't really safe, I think." He looked at the two of them. April looked anxious, but Evelyn looked kind of wistful.

"What are you thinking?" he asked.

Evelyn smiled. "I'm thinking...that I've spent a very long time traveling. And I don't want to travel anymore. I want...somewhere to call home. I want a place that is *mine*. A place to live. A place I can have friends. A place I can feel safe."

"I really agree," he said.

"Yeah, me too..." April murmured.

"I'm with this plan," Evelyn said. They both looked at April.

She sighed. "You're right. I'm anxious about moving, but that's just because new things scare me. I'm not sure if this place is really sustainable. We've been lucky so far, but yeah, that campground sounds better. And having more people we could trust around would make it a lot safer. I'm not exactly great at fighting or shooting."

"Okay then. That's a goal we'll be considering. For the time being, I at least want to go and check out a few of those structures near the watchtower that I passed on the way back here."

"Can I come?" Evelyn asked. "I've been dying to get out."

"April?" he asked, looking at her. "Would you feel okay here alone?"

She chewed her lower lip. "For how long?"

"A few hours, at least."

"I...yeah, I could handle that. I *have* pulled guard duty before," she replied.

"Thank you," Evelyn said.

David wondered if there was anything he could do to make her feel better, and suddenly remembered something. He got up and moved over to his pack, then pulled out the novel he'd salvaged from the watchtower.

"I got this for you, April," he said, coming back over to her. He handed her the fantasy novel and she accepted it, staring at it. "I thought you'd like it."

She stared at it for a long time, then looked up at him. "You remembered," she murmured.

He smiled. "Of course."

She put the paperback down on the table and leaped up suddenly, wrapping him in a tight, firm hug. "Thank you so much. You're so nice to me," she said softly.

He hugged her back. "I want you to be happy, April."

"You're doing a good job so far."

She held him for a while longer, then kissed him, released him, and sat back down.

"You're a real sweetheart," Evelyn said, smiling at him as he sat back down as well. They resumed eating their meals.

"Well, I try," he replied after a moment.

"You're succeeding," Evelyn said.

They kept eating.

# CHAPTER TEN

They walked to the campgrounds in silence.

David was surprised by how quickly it seemed to go by now that he was making the trip with someone else. With his girlfriend. He was still feeling big sparks of excitement and, honestly, disbelief whenever he thought that. Evelyn was amazing. Also an inhuman. His mind kept catching on that, and he felt kind of bad about it.

When he was growing up, he'd always thought there was this massive divide between humans and inhumans. It just seemed natural, and of course was perpetuated by many of the other humans he had come across. Some of that was people simply being misinformed, but most of it was just fear and hatred of something different.

To be fair, the squids and the nymphs were pretty different. They couldn't be called alien or unknowable, but from what he'd gathered they were a lot more insular and had adapted to live completely in the water and completely in the wild, respectively. He didn't think they were unapproachable, but he would say that they were different than the species that lived in the villages.

Although hey, maybe that was just ignorance speaking. He didn't actually *know* any squids or nymphs, and he'd only ever seen a few nymphs. Actually, come to think of it, he'd never directly spoken to either species.

But the goliaths, the reps, the jags, the AVs, even the half-undead wraiths, they really weren't that different than humans. Their biology gave them certain tendencies, certain strengths and weaknesses, but that was true of humans, too. It had taken him a while to see that there actually weren't differences inherent to the species.

Literally the only thing that was different about Evelyn was her size. If they were the same height, she'd pass for human. He was still kind of wrapping his head around that. Everyone had had anecdotes and stories and rumors about shit they'd seen or heard about the inhumans doing.

And it seemed pretty much to be universally bullshit.

An all-jag village was hardly any different than any all-human village. He imagined the biggest difference would be they wore fewer clothes.

Maybe he was thinking too much about this, but it was just a weird feeling that he was still experiencing the echoes of even now: the realization that something a *lot* of people believed and told you was actually just not true.

"Hey, there it is," Evelyn said.

He could see it, the fence and the row of buildings. "Yep."

"Wow, it looks in better condition than I remember," she murmured.

They walked up the path and in through the front gate, studying the fence as they went. "There's some holes," he said, pointing them out.

"Yeah. If we lived here, we'd have to fix them."

They came into the central path that connected all the buildings to each other and she looked around. "Huh, this is almost big enough to be the start of a new village."

"You think so?" he asked, realizing the same thing. He could see that. Most of the cabins could hold a family, some could hold more than that.

"Yeah. Definitely."

He thought about that as they looked around inside a few of the cabins, and then the large structure at the end. He imagined a dozen people here, three dozen people, fifty, all moving around, the air alive with conversation.

And it made him feel...strangely wistful.

He wanted that again, somewhere he felt safe with other people around. Good people, who were invested, and not just there because it was the most convenient. Not that he could necessarily blame most people for living like that.

Often, it was the only option.

They finished up their inspection of the area and then moved on.

He wanted to get to those cabins. He'd marked three cabins and a house on his map that he wanted to raid for supplies. They began heading off in that direction, moving through the trees, shooting the occasional zombie that crossed their path.

"What's your impression of April?" he asked after a bit.

"My impression? I think...she's tougher than she thinks she is. But she also definitely has some issues. I want her to be happy," Evelyn replied.

"Yeah, me too."

She laughed. "Well, *you* certainly have made her happy enough."

He chuckled awkwardly. "I guess so. She made me happy. You both have. This whole thing we have going is, uh...interesting."

"Oh is it now?" Evelyn asked.

"Yeah. What do you think?"

She paused, appearing to consider it. "You know what? I think it's sexy. I really like what we have going on here. I haven't had a lot of opportunities in my life to *feel* sexy, you know? To feel attractive, and also carefree. Those two things don't usually go together for me. Either I'm feeling carefree and unattractive, or I sometimes feel sexy but also really anxious that I'm fooling myself or whatever I have going on, I could lose it at any moment. But I don't feel that with you and April. I feel like you are just...*so* into me, and really natural and relaxed around you both."

"Well, I am *really* fucking into you," he replied.

"You certainly have been really deep into me," she murmured. "We should have sex again today. It feels *so* good."

"It feels fucking amazing," he agreed.

"Does it like, get you off, my size?" He hesitated, considering how to answer that. "I mean, like, I won't be mad if the answer's yes. I'm just curious."

"It does," he said. "It really does."

"Nice. I'm glad. I used to be worried about that, when I was younger. Like if I ever got with anyone who wasn't another goliath it would just be because goliaths turn them on. But now, as long as the relationship isn't entirely about that fact, like it's not the only reason you hooked up with me, I kind of like the idea. And I don't think that about you. And, to be totally honest, I'd be a hypocrite."

"Why's that?"

"Because the size difference kind of gets me off too. There's something really erotic about it," she admitted.

"Oh. Nice."

"Yeah. So I know what it feels like, and I like being able to make someone else feel like that, especially if I *really* like them. Which I do."

"I really like you too, Evie."

They were approaching the first cabin, he realized. These three were clustered together on a little plot of land. They both stopped as they approached.

"I hear something," David whispered.

Evelyn simply nodded, looking around. They had their guns out.

He spotted movement high up, on one of the roofs. A dark figure slipped into view, staring intently at them. He couldn't fully tell if it was a human or something else.

It was staring at them.

"David..." Evelyn whispered.

The figure let out a piercing shriek.

"Fuck!" he snapped, and fired off a shot.

It was a great one, hitting the thing, what he now realized must be a stalker, as they were the only ones to make that exact sound, right in the fucking face. It toppled forward and rolled off the roof, landing with a thud on the cold ground, but the damage was already done.

All around them, he heard movement and answering cries.

"Get ready," he growled.

They heard running footfalls and heavy panting and shifting foliage. And then, from around the cabins and the forest surrounding them came a dark tide of undead horrors. Mostly they were zombies, as was the standard fare for most attacks, but there were a solid eight stalkers mixed in, standing taller than the zombies, looking sturdier and more lethal.

"Fuck me," David muttered and fired off another shot, punching a hole in the head of one of the stalkers.

Overall, there had to be thirty undead heading for them.

"We can do this," Evelyn said. None were coming from behind, at least.

David threw it into high gear and began firing off shots as fast as he could manage.

They'd only brought pistols, leaving the shotgun with April.

He emptied the magazine and put down a dozen zombies and another stalker, then hastily reloaded and kept it up. He and Evelyn held their ground and killed as fast as they could, but the undead began to crowd in on them. David pistol-whipped one of them, breaking its nose and sending it stumbling back, then shooting it in the face.

Evelyn straight-up drop-kicked one of the stalkers when it got too close and he heard several of its bones break, both on the impact of her foot and the impact of it slamming into the ground several feet away. He briefly marveled again at her strength.

In the end, it was a bit of a close call, but they managed to take them all out without getting hit in return. David still wasn't exactly sure about the nature of this new virus. The thing was, everyone everywhere had the original virus. Or they probably did. It didn't affect about half of humans, and a quarter it morphed into one of the inhumans, and the rest it turned into zombies. But with this latest twist of the virus, he didn't know how at-risk he or anyone else was.

Since they already had the virus, could you just spontaneously begin turning into an undead now? Or was a scratch or a bite now the trigger?

Obviously not for some people. He'd been scratched more than once and although it hurt like a bitch, he'd kept it clean and nothing bad had come of it. And he'd also seen some people get bit, die, and come back as one of the new and improved types.

The only thing he knew for sure was that it was bullshit.

Wasn't there enough shit to deal with without this goddamned virus?

"You okay?" Evelyn asked.

"I'm fine. You?" he replied.

"I'm okay. Didn't get hit by anything. Damn, that was kind of nuts."

He laughed shakily. "Yeah."

They took the time to search all the bodies they'd made, checking pockets unhappily, trying to ignore the smell. As per usual, it wasn't exactly a fruitless endeavor, but it wasn't especially rewarding, either. They managed to pull a lighter, a knife, and a meager handful of bullets off the zombie corpses.

In a way, he was almost appreciative of the stalkers. Given they came from nymphs, who wore no clothes and had no pockets, they didn't need to be searched. Once *that* was finished, they began their search of the cabins.

They weren't very large structures, and one of them had a caved-in roof, and ice covered most surfaces in a thin layer. As they began their search, he found himself thinking of Ellie, and of Cait. Since coming to this region, he'd had both extremely good and extremely bad luck. He was mainly leaning towards good luck being the bigger of those two.

Sure, he'd had the village he was staying in for the winter collapse within a week, that was pretty shitty luck. But he had managed to hook up with *four* women since coming here.

*Four.*

This was basically the biggest explosion of sexual activity he'd had in his entire life. And three of them were inhumans. And *all* of them were *really* fucking hot! Ellie had just been...out of this world in terms of sex. He still kind of felt bad about that, because he absolutely loved sex with Evelyn, it was just...Ellie was...

He didn't want to say *better* at sex, more...

Fuck, he didn't know how else to say it.

Well, it wasn't like her ability to fuck was the only quality that Evelyn had. She was obviously a lot more emotionally available, and she was kinder than Ellie. It wasn't so much that Ellie was mean, (well, not most of the time at least), but obviously his jag...friend?

Were they friends? Acquaintance, he supposed, was the best phrase, because although they'd had sex three times now and she'd been pretty nice to him, given their previous interactions, he still wouldn't really call them friends per se. Or rather, he didn't think *she* would call them that. But yeah, it wasn't that she was mean, but she was obviously very guarded.

She probably had good reason to be.

Most people did, nowadays.

"Whoa, nice," Evelyn said.

"What?" he asked.

They were in the second cabin now, and she was searching the kitchen. He was on his hands and knees, looking under a bed across the room and seeing a whole lot of nothing.

"There's stuff in here," she said, ducking down as she stared into one of the cabinets. "Food. A jar of pickles. Some seasonings. Some cans."

He got up and moved over to her. She was taking

the supplies out and putting it on the counter above the cabinet.

"Sweet," he said, studying it. "This is a great find."

"Yes, I fucking love pickles," she replied, unscrewing the top and pulling out one of the pickle spears. She ate the whole thing in one go. "Oh my God, it's been like six months since I've had a pickle. These are *mine*."

"Fair enough," he replied, putting the other supplies into his backpack. The seasonings were going to be really nice.

They finished up their search, sweeping all three cabins, and didn't find a whole hell of a lot. Another blanket in decent condition, some more clothes, a bit more food, and a magazine of ammo that would fit their pistols someone had tucked away in a dresser a while ago. Once that was over with, they left the cabins, heading deeper into the forest, towards the house he had seen.

Houses, he found, on average tended to have better supplies hidden away in them. They made the walk in about five minutes, and as they approached the house, the front door suddenly opened up and a woman holding a pretty good-sized rifle stepped out.

"That's close enough," she said.

"Whoa, shit," Evelyn muttered as they came to a halt.

"What do you want?" the woman asked. David sized her up quickly: middle-aged, a bit grim, certainly looked like she'd shoot both of them if it came to it.

"We were just looking for supplies," David replied. "I thought this house was abandoned."

"It isn't."

"Yes...I can see that," he murmured.

They stared at each other for a moment as he tried to figure something out.

"Do you want to trade?" Evelyn asked.

"I'm not—" the woman began, but hesitated and glanced back over her shoulder. Probably someone else deeper in the house talking to her. She said something sharply, but he couldn't tell what it was, they were too far away. She carried on a hasty conversation with someone, then stared at them reluctantly. "I'd be willing to trade food for a favor."

"What favor?" David asked, perking up. They needed food.

"One of ours is missing. She went to the village earlier today and she should have been back by now. You find her and get her back here safely, we'll give you some food."

He looked at Evelyn, who nodded. "Okay, deal. What's she look like? What's her name?"

"Ashley. She's blonde, a bit on the leaner side, short hair. She'll be wearing white clothing," the woman responded.

"Okay, we'll find her," David replied.

The woman nodded, then closed the door.

"Come on, we should hurry," he said, and they hurried off towards the village.

…

"I really didn't feel like coming back to this place," David muttered as they finally caught sight of the village.

"Same," Evelyn replied unhappily.

There were now some really bad memories here. Even looking at it made him flash back to the night he'd woken up to chaos and getting hit in the head and watching the place burn as zombies tore people apart in a tide of death.

"Wait, do you hear that?" Evelyn whispered as they drew closer.

He did. A voice, a guy's voice, and he didn't sound friendly. They crept close with as much stealth as they could manage, which wasn't a whole lot given Evelyn's size. Despite that, they managed to get up to a big hole in the outer wall and peered into the street beyond. It was still littered with corpses, only this time there were a baker's dozen people standing there.

One of them had to be the woman they were looking for, Ashley. She was blonde with short hair, wearing closer to a grayish set of clothes, a coat and some cargo pants, and pale gray boots. All the rest were guys dressed in a random mishmash of clothes.

Thieves, they had to be.

There was a good chance they were part of the group of assholes who'd caused the downfall of the village.

"How do we do this?" he whispered.

"Shit, I'm not sure. I guess...try to scare them off?" Evelyn replied.

"How do we do that? You're certainly capable of being intimidating, but there's like a dozen of them and, well...goliaths *do* go down typically just as easily as everyone else if you put a bullet in their brain," he murmured.

She sighed. "Good point."

As they watched, the man nearest to the woman stepped forward and shoved her suddenly. She grunted and landed hard on the ground.

"Fuck," he snapped, raising his pistol. "Okay,

I'm going to head to the left side, try to find cover behind one of the shacks so I have a good angle. Stay here, cover me. Start firing when I start firing, take down as many as you can as fast as you can."

"I...okay," she replied.

He gave her a quick kiss and then slipped through the wall.

Well, this was going to be really dangerous. They were all facing away from him presently, looking in pretty much every other direction. He didn't relish the thought of killing people, but he instantly knew what he was looking at: monsters. Everything about them screamed thieves, murderers, rapists.

Sociopathic assholes, basically. They weren't just stealing to survive, they weren't killing in self defense, these were the kind of people who got off on hurting other people. Sadistic assholes who had zero regard for human life.

David got into place.

Okay, it was the moment of truth.

"Stay the fuck down!" he heard someone scream, and another voice cried out in pain

He leaned around the corner, now having probably the best view he was going to get of the whole mess. The leader was standing over the woman, and the others were crowding around her.

"Hold her the fuck down," he said, his voice carrying really well in the still air.

Three of the others began to move forward and he started messing with his pants, staring down at the woman laying on the ground, who tried to leap to her feet but was basically leaped upon by the other three.

Fuck, it was go time.

He aimed and fired, putting a round through the back of one thief's head and sending him tumbling forward. He shifted aim and managed to cap another one as they all began twisting around, both trying to get out of the line of fire and also find out where it was coming from. Another good headshot and another bastard went down.

The leader spun around. "What the fuck–" he began, and then a bullet entered his mouth and punched through the back of his skull in a spray of blood.

"Holy shit," David whispered. Evelyn was a good goddamn shot.

It fell into chaos after that.

People ran, returned fire, and things became more confusing as the woman snatched up a pistol from the dead leader and began firing on the others, screaming as she did so. David shot another man in the neck, put two rounds into someone's chest, and managed to cap another guy in the face as he leaned out from behind a building to try and return fire.

He saw a few of the men run away and doubted they were coming back anytime soon. He emptied his magazine and reloaded after that initial firefight, and before long, the shooting died down, then died off. He and Evelyn waited, listening intently.

Suddenly he heard a grunt, followed by running footsteps, then three shots, a scream, and the thump of a body. Then yelling in pain.

Then another gunshot and nothing.

Finally, a voice called out. "Who saved my ass?"

"Uh...me," David said.

"Who are you?"

"David...can I come out?"

"Yeah."

"There's someone else with me. A goliath, she's going to come out too, okay?"

"Fine."

He slowly came out, wary of any survivors. Counting up the bodies, he saw that eight of them had been killed. He was reasonably sure the other four had fled. Evelyn joined him and together they walked down the road to where the blonde woman was getting up and brushing herself off. She looked more annoyed than anything else.

"Are you okay?" Evelyn asked.

"Some cuts and scrapes and my clothes are a fucking mess, but I'll be fine," she replied, then she looked down at the leader, who was the nearest corpse, and kicked his head angrily. "Fucking stupid bastard," she growled. "Who are you?"

"Just some survivors from the village. Your family sent us after we found your house out in the woods," David explained.

"Oh. That makes sense, I guess. Well, thank you." She looked at them, then looked around at the ruined village surrounding them. "So, you were here when it went down, too?"

"Yeah. We barely got out."

"You staying in a cabin or house or something?"

"Yeah, a cabin out in the woods with another woman we found here," Evelyn replied.

"Okay." She studied them, seeming to size them up. "Would you be willing to help me look for something? That's why I'm here."

"What is it?" David asked.

"A locket. *My* locket. I want it. I left it behind in an apartment deeper in. I'll split whatever supplies we find while we're here," she said.

David looked at Evelyn, who nodded. "Yeah, okay."

"Why don't you let me help you with those

wounds. You can't just leave them open like that," Evelyn said as she reached for her medical kit.

"You sound like my mother...okay, I appreciate it," Ashley replied.

While Evelyn tended to her, David began patting down the corpses for supplies. These, at least, yielded more than the zombies. Though not as much as he would have liked. Only three of them had been armed, and one with a pistol so shitty it had apparently broken in the fall. The others had probably run off with guns of their own.

David managed to scrounge up a bit of ammo and one pistol, a little revolver that took thirty-eight caliber rounds. He managed to find a bit of medical supplies on them, one had a knife, and some of them had bits of food. Mostly flat, rectangular tins packed with some kind of meat or fish.

When Evelyn was finished helping Ashley, they split the findings and then she began leading them deeper into the village, towards the place she had been staying.

"So what's your story?" she asked.

David told her what he could think of about how he and Evelyn had met and all the things that had happened since then, keeping it simple. While he was telling the story, she took him to one of the more intact apartment buildings and they got inside, moving slowly and carefully as they checked around for anything dangerous.

"So what about you?" he asked after telling his story.

"I've been living here for about two months," she replied. "With my family. My mom and dad and little brother. We moved from farther north. We were headed another place even farther south than this, but we ran into a lot of problems and eventually I think my parents were just too tired to keep going, and so we decided to settle here for now. Talk about bad luck."

"Yeah," David murmured.

"So now we're out in that house with another older couple and a kid they've kind of adopted. He lost his parents so it's...really depressing. But we're getting along, I guess. For now, anyway." She sighed as they made their way up some stairs and down a corridor. "Man, this whole thing sucks, and now winter's pretty much here."

David and Evelyn murmured in agreement.

It wasn't exactly the greatest situation.

They came to a door and she opened it up. "Okay, I'm going to go find my locket. You two should search the area. We grabbed some stuff, but not everything, and I'm not sure if anyone's been here. We can split the supplies."

"Okay," David said.

He pointed Evelyn to the living room area while he went into the kitchen and Ashley went down the hallway to, presumably, the bedrooms. He worked fast, opening up all the cabinet doors and the drawers and hunting through it all. A lot of them were empty, either having never contained anything to begin with or they'd been cleared out by Ashley's family during the evacuation, but not all of them were.

He found a lot of cans, fifteen in all, a random collection of fruits, vegetables, and meats. He also found some seasonings and spices, and some sliced beef in the fridge, which had lost power, but it was pretty cold in the apartment so it probably wasn't actually bad yet. It was wrapped up and tied with twine. He set it all on the counter.

Evelyn just turned up a few blankets and some shotgun shells from under the couch. David found himself wondering how they'd gotten there. After several more minutes, Ashley returned, looking pleased with herself. She had a faded golden locket around her neck and her backpack seemed heavier than before.

"Okay, I've got everything I needed. What'd you find?" she asked.

"Some food, a few shotgun shells, a few blankets," he replied.

"Okay, sweet. Let's see."

She let them keep the shells and the blanket, and took most of the food after he felt compelled to tell her that their reward for this was going to be more food. So that all seemed to balance out. Once that was sorted out, they started heading back.

"Is there a story behind the locket?" Evelyn asked.

"Yeah. Short of it is the first boy I ever loved gave it to me almost ten years ago now. We parted ways eventually, a few things necessitated it, but I still love him, and want to remember him. It's the only thing I really carry with me that I don't want to replace, that I really can't replace," Ashley explained.

"That's sweet," Evelyn murmured.

"I like to think so. Come on, let's get home so my family can stop worrying."

# CHAPTER ELEVEN

The rest of the day went pretty smoothly.

They walked back to Ashley's family's place and returned her, (and got to watch her and her mother argue for a few minutes while her father got their reward).

They managed to get their hands on probably another three days' worth of food, which was...not exactly great, but definitely good. After parting ways, the two headed back home, figuring they'd left April alone for long enough.

David was extremely grateful to see that she'd not only been okay, having run into no problems while they were out, but she'd taken some initiative and had begun building up a supply of clean water, melting and boiling snow from around the area.

He stayed in for the night after that, tidying the place up a bit more with Evelyn and April, and getting to know them a bit better. Eventually, night fell, and the three of them went to sleep, again curled up together on the nest of blankets.

And the sleep was a good, and deep, and satisfying one.

...

When David woke up, he was, like most mornings, extremely horny.

Evelyn was already awake, he realized as he shifted around, looking for some source of satisfaction. She was at the fireplace.

"Hey," he murmured, looking at her.

"Hey...you look like you want something," she

replied.

"Yeah. Uh...I'm super fucking horny."

She giggled. "Sorry, I already masturbated when I woke up. You looked dead asleep, so I didn't want to wake you. And I will fuck you, if you want, but I think April would appreciate the dick more right now," she said.

"Oh..." He looked over at April, who was slowly stirring. "Yes..." He found a bottle of lube nearby and grabbed it, then gently shook her.

"What?" she murmured.

"Are you horny?" he asked.

"Yes. Like, *really* horny. I was having a fuck dream. Will you fuck me?" she asked.

"Yes. Get on your hands and knees."

"Okay."

She did so, pushing herself up into that awesome position, looking extremely sexy, and he quickly rubbed himself down and then got behind her.

"Holy shit, April," he murmured as he looked down at her.

"What?" she asked, sounding a little startled.

"Your fucking ass and tail are so hot," he said, then settled one hand around the top of her tail, making her gasp and jerk in surprise, and with his other hand guided his cock to the entrance of her extremely tight rep vagina.

"Oh, thank–ah!–you," she moaned as he penetrated her.

He groaned loudly as he slipped into her. David shifted his other hand to settle on one of her small, firm hips and began running his first hand up and down her tail, making her moan even louder. He began sliding in and out of her, feeling that *incredible* drag on his cock from her insanely tight pussy.

She felt so strange inside, but in a really good way. So smooth, but different from sex with any of the other types of women he'd been with. The texture of her pussy was just...slicker, and it felt fucking awesome.

"Oh fuck, April," he groaned, pounding her harder as his morning lust began to overtake him.

"Yes...fuck...yes! *Give it to me!*" she screamed.

He pounded her brains out for another sixty seconds before she began coming, and she screamed in wild, rapturous release as she orgasmed. David let out a loud groan and then gripped her hips firmly with both hands, his grasp tight, fingertips digging in as he began thrusting hard and fast into her, emptying his cock inside of her, pumping her full of his seed as he grunted furiously.

He felt totally entwined with her, enraptured by the overwhelmingly powerful pleasure their sex was giving him as he came into her.

When he was finished, he felt a lot more awake and aware.

"Damn," he whispered, and pulled out of her.

She groaned and fell forward, resting back on the pillows. "Yeah..." she said tiredly. "That was so good."

"Yep," he agreed as he got to his feet.

He moved over to the washing water and began the process of cleaning himself up. It always helped finish the wake-up process in the mornings. After that, he and, eventually, April, went through their morning routine. They washed up, dressed, and ate the breakfast that Evelyn had so kindly made for them.

"What are we doing today?" Evelyn asked.

"I had, um...a thought," April said. They both

looked at her. She looked down at her plate, pushing her food around, looking anxious. "I was thinking...you were right. We should think about moving somewhere safer. I just don't want things to change, and the idea of leaving this place makes me scared, now that I'm actually here and after everything that happened. But that's not really sustainable or realistic, so...if you'd indulge me, I'd like one of you to take me to the campgrounds you're talking about and show me around. I need to actually get out there and make the walk there, but I don't want to do it alone."

"I can do that," David offered.

"It wouldn't be a bother? I know there's no real reason to go back there yet and this wouldn't provide any real benefit to us, it'd be indulging me..."

"It's really okay, April," he said. "You feeling okay about this matters to me. It's worth it. We'll walk there, I'll show you around, then we can walk back. It'll take like an hour at most," David replied, smiling at her.

She gave him a tentative smile back. "Thank you."

"You're welcome."

"Don't be afraid to speak up for yourself with us, April," Evelyn said. "You can trust us. I know that there's been a lot of...well, an air of 'cut your losses and leave the weak behind' in our society, but you really don't have to worry about that here with us. It's...okay to show weakness and vulnerability around us. We help each other."

"I believe you, I *do* trust both of you, I just...I'm still adjusting. And I'm always going to have a certain amount of awkwardness and hesitation. It's just...who I am. But really, genuinely, from the bottom of my heart, thank you," she said. "The fact that you are willing to help me, and watch out for me like this...it's honestly probably the greatest gift I've ever received."

They kept eating, and David felt happy.

It was good to have relationships like this.

It might be the most valuable thing in his life, in this horrible new world they found themselves in. It certainly felt like it, in this moment.

...

David and April both armed themselves with pistols, and set out not much later.

It was a gray day outside, but there didn't seem to be a storm on the horizon. Everything was still covered in a relatively fresh layer of snow from the huge blizzard, and had that eerily beautiful sheen to it. Nice to look at, less nice to actually have to walk through. April put on several layers of clothing, and he was reminded that she had other reasons for hating going outside.

He hated being cold, but she *really* wasn't supposed to be out in this kind of temperature. So he made sure to keep a brisk pace and dispatch any wandering zombies that got too close quickly. They managed to reach the campgrounds before too long.

"Wow, so this is it?" April murmured as they made their way in.

"Yep," David replied. He led her down the initial path and into the main area. "We could stay in any one of these cabins, or...we could stay in there," he said, pointing at the three-story structure at the left end of the path.

"Wow," she whispered. "That looks pretty

secure. All this does. And the fencing...yeah, I have to say, I think you're right. This place is a *way* better place to stay than in the basement of an old, abandoned cabin."

"I'm glad you agree," David said. He took her hand and began guiding her towards the main structure. She smiled at him and laced their fingers together.

"You're really...touchy-feely," she said.

"Is that a problem? I can stop," he replied.

"No! No, not at all. I love it. I'm just...surprised. I guess most of the relationships I've had aren't exactly...romantic. They were more, uh, functional, I suppose you could say. And it's really interesting to be touchy-feely with someone from another species. It's really nice. I like how you feel when you touch me, when I touch you, when we hold hands."

"I feel the same way," he said.

They headed inside. The three-story building still had furniture, thankfully, so when they moved in *that* would at least be taken care of, for the most part. There was some kind of office and reception area taking up most of the first floor, as well as a bathroom and even a basement area that largely seemed relegated to storage.

They'd definitely have to sort through that. The second floor had what might have been a kind of lounge, with a few big windows that looked out over the area, and a kitchen and dining area. There was also a little side room that looked empty. The third floor had two bedrooms, one master size, one regular sized.

He showed the whole thing to April, letting her get a feel for the place.

Then they made their way back down the stairs,

and David froze as he looked out the front window. His eyes caught immediately upon a figure, like your sleeve snagging on a nail in passing, ripping you abruptly to a halt. April noticed the lone figure as well and made a sound of surprised fear. And then he relaxed.

"It's okay," he said. "I know her."

"Oh...okay, wow, that scared the shit out of me," April murmured.

"Come on."

They headed outside, towards the blue-furred figure, who seemed to be waiting for them in the cold daylight.

"Hello, Ellie," David said as they stepped outside.

"Hi, David. I assume you're April," Ellie replied.

"Yeah," April said.

"What can I do for you?" David asked.

"I've been looking for you. I want your help with something." He noticed she very specifically didn't say *need*, but *want*. She wanted his help.

Interesting.

"What is it?" he asked.

"There's some farms east of the abandoned village. They're still largely functional and I have a deal set up with them. I help them with problems, they supply me with food. I've got a big problem and I figured you'd both like the opportunity to help some people and the opportunity to get yourselves some real food, and maybe make an extremely important connection," Ellie explained.

"I'd love the opportunity," David said. "What's the job?"

"There's a giant around, causing problems, scaring and, in some cases, killing people. We're going to kill it," Ellie said.

David felt his heart skip a beat. A giant? Fuck.

They were the monster version of a goliath. They were like ten feet tall and dangerous as all fucking hell. Well, that was certainly worth doing, and they *needed* food. That wasn't really optional. So he was going to do this.

"You have a deal," he said.

"Great! Let's go," Ellie replied, then turned and began walking off.

"Wait. I need to drop April off first, see her home safely," David said.

Ellie stopped and turned back around. She eyed April. "She's a big girl, I'm sure she can get home on her own."

"No," David said.

"Oh, come on," Ellie replied.

"I can probably make it fine..." April murmured.

"This isn't negotiable, Ellie. You want my help, we make time for this. It's on the way anyway, it shouldn't be more than a few minutes of a delay," he said firmly.

Ellie sighed. "Okay, fine. Let's go."

"I'm sorry," April said as they started leaving the campground.

"It's fine, April. This is important to me. *You* are important to me. I'm not going to just leave you out here on your own. I know how terrifying that can be," he said.

"I...thank you. I *really* appreciate this," she replied, looking embarrassed, which just made him feel bad for her.

"You're welcome."

They walked back through the forest, the way they'd come, and she stuck close to him. David felt a bit torn. On the one hand, he did understand Ellie's point of view, which she had managed to convey in just a few simple words.

Ellie was obviously a loner and a survivor, and very hardcore. April was basically antithetical to her. Ellie was no doubt of the mindset that April should toughen up, and David didn't entirely think she was wrong.

But he'd also seen a *lot* of damage done to people who had that shit hammered into them, screamed at them, repeated over and over and over: Get over it. Toughen up. Quit being a little bitch.

You could help build someone up without being a fucking asshole about it.

Honestly, it rarely seemed to even work. The kind of people tough love actually worked on, tended not to need it, ironically. David did want to help her, to rebuild her confidence, but not at the cost of her happiness.

They reached the cabin before too long.

"*This* is where you're staying?" Ellie asked.

"For now," David replied as they approached.

Evelyn was out back, chopping wood. She straightened up as she saw them approaching, favoring them with a beautiful smile.

"You must be Ellie," Evelyn said. "You must be the one that fucked my boyfriend during the snowstorm."

David glanced at Ellie. He had to admit, the look of hesitation and the tinge of actual fear on her features was oddly satisfying.

"Yes..." Ellie replied slowly.

Evelyn laughed. "He said you were amazing. Thanks for helping him, and making him come. He loves that."

Ellie looked at David, then she laughed, and it looked like it surprised her to do so, like she wasn't expecting the laugh. He laughed, too.

"So what's up?" Evelyn asked.

"Ellie and I are going to go kill a giant," David replied.

Evelyn's features fell, and a look of anxiety passed across her face. "Oh...that sounds very dangerous. Maybe I should help..."

David glanced at Ellie. "I think we can handle it."

"If you're sure..."

"Ellie's pretty hardcore."

"All right. I guess I'll stick around here. I *did* hear something moving around out there," Evelyn murmured unhappily, and scanned the forest.

And now it was *his* turn to be anxious.

Nonetheless, he said his goodbyes to Evelyn and April, giving each of them a kiss and a hug, then grabbed a bit more ammo and, after a moment's consideration, the shotgun. It seemed like something worth having when fighting a giant.

And then they set out.

...

"So you're really in a relationship with a goliath, huh?" Ellie asked as they walked on.

"Yeah...is that so surprising?" David replied.

"I mean yeah, in my experience, goliaths tend to date goliaths. Don't get me wrong, I don't disapprove or anything. I think it's great. People should be happy. Is April part of the relationship or..." she trailed off.

"Sort of," David replied, considering it. "I mean,

I guess, functionally speaking, we're in a three-way relationship. We all trust each other and have sex with each other."

"Sounds nice," Ellie murmured. She hesitated. "Are you mad at me?"

"Yeah, kind of," he replied.

She stopped and looked back at him. "Why?"

"You were rude to April."

She opened her mouth as an expression that suggested she was going to immediately leap to her own defense came across her face, but she didn't say anything. She closed it and stared at him. Behind her, her tail twitched.

"I'm sorry," she said. "You're right."

"You should apologize to her the next time you see her."

Ellie sighed. "Yeah, okay. I guess I was just..."

"Just what?" he asked. She looked oddly guilty.

"Testing you again."

"What do you mean 'again'?" he asked.

"I wanted to make sure you weren't full of shit. You're the kind of guy who seems too good to be true, you know that?"

"What, why?"

"Because you're not selfish. Because you're nice. Because you help people for no other reason than to help them. Because you're honest. Do you know how many goddamned people I've met who have a 'fuck you, got mine' mentality? People who are just out for themselves. Liars, thieves, assholes. Too many, and most of the rest would rather not get involved."

"Okay. How were you testing me?"

"When I gave you the supplies to give to the family, and told you to give most of it to them, I followed you. And when I gave you the location of my stash, you could have taken more. All of it. But you didn't. You've been helping people. And you seem to have a good relationship with April and Evelyn. And that just...I had to know."

"Why?" he asked.

"Because people like you are extremely rare, and worth knowing. I don't make friends easily, and it's good to have, you know, allies. People I can rely on, in case of emergency..."

"Is that why you fucked me?" he asked.

"No! I wasn't–that wasn't manipulation, David. I fucked you because I liked you." She heaved a sigh. "Fuck, I'm so bad at this."

David relaxed. She hadn't actually done anything wrong, at least from what he could see, and he believed her. And, well, it was nice knowing that someone thought he was a good person. He also felt kind of bad for her, and sympathized with her: it could be really hard to make friends. He imagined it could be even harder to make friends if you had her type of persona.

She started walking again suddenly and he moved to keep up with her.

"Ellie, if it helps, I understand. And I want to be your friend," he said.

"Do you really?" she asked.

"Why would you ask that?"

She glanced over at him. "I'm a useful ally to have...and a great fuck. I know that much."

"Ellie–" he said, staring back at her. "You-you can't just snap back and forth between being vulnerable and apologetic to being overly confident and suspicious!"

She frowned and stared ahead for several seconds. Her tail was twitching hard again. "You're right. I'm sorry. Again. Fuck, I said I was bad at this." She stopped suddenly, and he nearly tripped as he stopped as well.

Ellie offered him her hand. "Friends?"

He grasped it firmly, shook it. "Friends," he confirmed.

"Thank you."

They started walking again.

...

David had heard a few references to a farm somewhere in the region, but he had no idea that they were so close to the village. He saw huge, empty fields surrounded by a large, ten-foot-tall fence topped with barbed wire. It looked pretty secure.

"How many people live here?" he asked.

"I'm not sure. A few dozen, at least. There's several families here. They're very secure and know their shit. No one fucks with them, because they control the biggest, most readily available source of food in the whole region," Ellie explained.

"Yeah, I'd want to stay on their good side," he murmured. "Do they take advantage of that?"

"Actually, no. For as long as I've known them, they've been pretty reasonable."

"Well that's good...so where's the giant?"

"Last I heard, due northeast. Closer to the river. Come on."

They got to a road leading towards the river and began walking up it. The more they walked and the silence dragged on, the more anxious David became. He'd only ever seen two giants before, and in neither of those instances had he actually attempted to fight one.

Other people had been there during the first time, people who were good at fighting and killing, and the second time it had been from afar and there'd been no real confrontation of any kind.

And now he was going to attempt to kill one with just one other person.

Granted, Ellie was obviously a very capable fighter, but...now he was beginning to regret leaving Evelyn behind. She would have been a helpful ally in this fight. Too late now though, he told himself. What was done was done, and the situation was what it was. He was just going to have to make this happen.

They walked along for another five minutes before Ellie stopped and made him stop with an outstretched hand. Her cat ears were perked up and she was looking off to the right, towards a rise in the landscape.

"Come on," she whispered. "Quietly."

He followed her, padding along as quietly as he could up the incline, winding his way with her through the dead trees until they both were crouching at the crest of the hill. The area below was a large clearing in the forest, and in that clearing was...

"Wow, that is big," David whispered.

"Yep. If I had my rifle, I could take it out now, but my rifle is broken right now. So...instead, we are going to stand at the top of this hill and fire bullets into that thing, making it run towards us, and we will continue to fire bullets into it until it dies. Sound good?" she asked.

"I...yeah, okay," he replied.

"Good. Then let's do it."

They both stood up and pulled out their pistols.

His heart was starting to hammer in his chest as he really got a look at the thing. It was a good nine or ten feet tall, and pretty built. It looked like it could bench-press a truck. Its skin was ashy gray and it wore just bare tatters of clothing. Right as they took aim for it, the thing took notice of them, and turned dead, white eyes on them.

Its face was a mask-like sneer of fury and blind rage.

They opened fire.

The pistols barked in the still air and the rounds began impacting on its large body. The thing let out a roar that sent birds flying from trees and seemed to shake the area, then began barreling towards them with a terrifying speed.

David forced himself to keep his aim steady. He squeezed the trigger steadily, aiming with as much precision as he could muster. He missed as often as he connected, which embarrassed the hell out of him given the size of the target...or would have if he wasn't so fucking terrified right now.

He put two rounds into its chest, missed the next three shots, put another in its neck, missed, one in its shoulder, missed two more. The thing was moving so *fast* for something so big!

It reached the base of the hill and slowed slightly as it began coming up for them.

"Take it down!" Ellie snapped.

They both reloaded and kept firing. It took a dozen bullets, then two dozen, and still it was coming. It bled dark blood sluggishly from the wounds, but neither of them were making that all-important killshot. He'd *seen* two bullets enter its head so far, but clearly its skull was too thick or its brain was harder to take down.

His pistol ran dry a second time and now it was closer than ever.

He went to reload again but fumbled and dropped the magazine.

"Fuck!" he snapped, and it was almost upon them.

He dropped the pistol, abandoning his efforts with it, and instead snatched the shotgun from where it hung off his shoulder. Bringing it up, he aimed right for its face and squeezed the trigger. The gun thundered and shook in his grasp and the giant stopped and stumbled back a step...*and then it kept coming.*

"Are you fucking–" he screamed in fear and anger and fired again.

This shot tore away a piece of its head and sent it stumbling back several steps, then caused it to fall back down the hill.

When it hit the bottom, it wasn't moving.

"Wow," David whispered, his hands shaking as he lowered the shotgun. "Fuck me."

Ellie walked down the hill without a word and stopped an appreciable distance away from the corpse, then put three rounds into its head. She walked back up to join him. "Come on, David," she said, and began walking back.

He stared at the body a few seconds longer, then retrieved his pistol and the magazine he'd dropped, turned and began following after her.

# CHAPTER TWELVE

"Wait, what are we doing exactly?" David asked.

They'd been walking back towards the farms for a few minutes now in silence, and he was feeling a little shell-shocked after the encounter. It had been a pretty damned terrifying one. So he wasn't paying as close of attention as he should. She'd taken them off the main path, down a side one, and now, he saw, towards an abandoned cabin.

"You made a request," Ellie replied as she approached the cabin.

"I...did?" he asked, trying to figure out what the fuck she was talking about.

"Yep. Wait here."

She moved around the cabin's exterior in a quick circle, then walked inside and moved around for a bit, then came back to the door and stared at him intently. "I very specifically heard you say 'fuck me', and I think that's a fair request. So get in here."

"Uh...oh, wow," he said as it came together. That wasn't what he'd meant but...well, he'd certainly take it if she was offering it.

He walked into the cabin and she closed and locked the door behind her, then she pushed him up against the door and stared at him with a sly smile on her face. "*You* are becoming more attractive the more time I spend with you," she said, running a fingertip down one side of his face.

"I, uh, really?" he managed, his heart starting to beat harder in his chest again, although for a completely different reason this time around.

"Yes. Really." She kissed him.

Well, she was *definitely* attractive to him.

He responded immediately, hugging her to him, kissing her passionately. He ran his hands over her soft, warm body, feeling her fur, then down to her tail, which was twitching madly now. She gasped when he touched it, when he wrapped his fingers around it, and gave it a small squeeze.

She smiled into the kiss. "I really like it when you do that, which you should count yourself really goddamned fucking lucky for, because I don't let hardly anyone else alive do that," she said, her lips brushing his as she spoke.

"Then I count myself really lucky," he replied.

"Good." She kissed him again, and he began guiding her slowly across the room, back towards a bed in the corner.

He was going to enjoy this deeply.

David found himself even more excited than usual as they began stripping. It was probably all the fear and adrenaline he'd built up during the fight, and now something else exciting was happening, so it had that extra infusion of emotional intensity.

And apparently Ellie was feeling it too, because as soon as they were nude, she grabbed him and shoved him back onto the bed, then mounted him in one smooth motion.

"You are amazingly fit," he said as she reached between them and grasped his cock, which felt about as hard as tempered steel right then.

"Yep," she agreed. "And I don't want to deal with foreplay right now, so we're fucking."

"Okay."

She laughed, then gasped as she began to penetrate herself with his cock. The whole world seemed to immediately begin drifting away as he slid into her pussy and he felt himself become enveloped in that tight, wet perfection. She was very wet and he slipped right in, and how fucking *hot* she was!

Jags, he was finding, had hotter pussies than humans, goliaths, or reps. And he groaned loudly, arching his back and grabbing her hips as she began bouncing on him once she was comfortably in place.

"Oh fuck, Ellie..." he moaned loudly.

"You cannot get enough of me, can you?" she asked, panting, as she rode him. Her firm, amazingly hot tits bounced in rhythm with her motions as she put her hips and thighs to use.

"Yes. Fuck. Oh my–*fuck, Ellie...*" he groaned, feeling almost incoherent with insane lust.

He started thrusting up into her. He wanted, no, he *needed* to be fucking her, not just having sex with her but goddamned pounding her fucking brains out and screwing her like they were in heat. Ellie started crying out as he drove his cock up into her hard and fast, and he wanted to make her scream even louder.

He grabbed her ass and fucked her brains out, making the bed shake and making her really bounce on his dick.

"Oh *yes, David! Oh fuck! Yes! Don't stop!*" she begged.

He reached up and grabbed her tits after a while, loving the feel of them, how great they felt, bare and soft and warm and firm in his grasp. After another minute or so, he suddenly hugged her to him, then flipped them both over.

"Oh fuck!" she cried in surprise as she ended up on her back.

He immediately resumed fucking her as she spread her legs out for him, really fucking pounding her into the bed, making it creak and shake violently. He listened to her scream and shout, pant and moan and beg for more in desperate, almost mindless pleasure. At one point, she began to orgasm, and she really started screaming her brains out. He groaned loudly, grunting as he basked in the raw pleasure of continuing to fuck her orgasming vagina.

The fact that this was completely bareback enhanced it by a factor of about a thousand.

When she was done, he suddenly got up onto his knees, grabbed one of her legs, and shoved it up. He shifted a bit more, so that he had the best position and, holding her leg up, he resumed drilling the fuck out of her pussy.

*"Oh my fucking shit, David! Fuck! PLEASE MORE!"* she screamed.

"You want more, you slut?" he asked.

*"Yes! OH FUCK YES! MORE! I WANT MORE!"* she begged, incoherent with pure sexual satisfaction and raw, uncut pleasure.

He reached down and started rubbing her clit as he continued pounding the fuck out of her. She thrashed and shrieked wildly and he had her coming again within another thirty seconds.

This time he didn't hold back. He kept fucking her pussy and soon he was coming along with her, shooting his load directly into her jag pussy, filling her up, joining her in shared bliss, blindingly powerful, overwhelming sexual rapture.

He felt his seed leaving him in hard contractions, spurting into her, pumping into that sweet pussy of hers over and over again, sending out waves of rapturous pink ecstasy. They came and moaned and yelled together.

When he was finished, David pulled out of her and sat down on the edge of the bed, staring at the floor, getting his breath back.

"How are you this good at sex?" Ellie panted. "That was...oh my God," she whispered.

"I think I was just, uh, in the zone," David replied. He ran his hand through his hair, then popped his neck. "Wow, that was good."

"Yeah, I'll fucking say. God, those two girls must fucking love you."

"Well, that'd be nice. Right now, we all like each other," he replied.

"When you're dicking them, they love you," Ellie said, she shifted slightly, then groaned. "Wow, that was some fuck. Just...ugh, wow." She shifted again, then looked down at herself. "You made a big mess."

"So did you," he replied.

"Yeah, fair point." She sighed. "I don't want to get up, but we have a bounty to collect on..."

David laid down beside her suddenly and hugged her to him. "We don't have to go yet. We can stay here for a bit, like this," he said.

"I...hmm...okay," she murmured uncertainly, hugging him back.

"Do you not want to do this?"

"I do. It just feels..." she hesitated.

"Like what?"

"I don't know, surrendering somehow. Being weak."

"It doesn't have to. I guess it would be if you were around someone you couldn't trust, someone who might want to take advantage of you at some point. Except I'm not going to do that."

"Everyone says that. Especially people who are going to take advantage of you," Ellie pointed out.

David sighed. "Yeah, I know. All I have are my actions. How do you feel about me?"

Ellie was quiet for a moment. "I trust you enough to have sex with you more than once. I don't think you're going to get weird about it, and I'm...reasonably sure you aren't going to do something to take advantage of me somehow. But this isn't...it doesn't come naturally to me. So yeah, doing something like cuddling is actually a lot harder than fucking. Which, still, you should consider yourself lucky, I hardly fuck anyone."

"I still consider myself lucky," he replied. "And, you know, I don't want to make you uncomfortable. We can stop whenever you want."

"That's the thing, I *like* this. A lot. I just don't like that I like it. Weakness and vulnerability aren't exactly rewarded in this world."

"No, they aren't," he murmured. "But if you find the right people, you can be vulnerable around them, and it won't cost you. It will help you."

"That'd be nice," she said quietly.

They laid there in comfortable silence for several more minutes, until finally Ellie began to rouse herself and got up. "Okay, *now* I want to get up because both you blew a huge load in me and I really want to take care of it, and if I'm inert for too long I start to go crazy."

"Okay," he said, "it was really nice while it lasted."

"Yes, it was," she murmured, sounding like she was begrudgingly admitting something.

They both used water from bottles in their packs and rags to wash up, and then they pulled their clothes back on. After that, they left the cabin and hit the road, heading back towards the farms, and towards their reward.

And, ideally, a link to regular access to food for

him and Evelyn and April.

"Ellie, I was wondering...would you be interested in staying with us at all? We're going to be moving to those campgrounds you found me in with April, so we'll have more room."

"No," Ellie said, almost immediately.

"You didn't even think about it."

"I know. I...don't settle down. But, well, I'd be willing to help you out if you're ever in any kind of serious trouble, or swing by and get laid. Or watch you fuck Evelyn. I have to admit, I really want to see you fucking her. She is *so* much taller than you."

"Yeah, almost a foot and a half," David murmured. "It is wicked hot, or at least, I mean, I think it is. I certainly enjoy it."

"I bet." She paused. "I'm sorry, it isn't anything personal. I *do* like you, I just...don't settle down."

"Okay," he said.

They walked on for a few more seconds.

"That was easy," Ellie said eventually.

"What was?"

"You just...accepted that. I mean, so many people would have kept pushing, kept trying."

"That would be rude."

"I know, that doesn't seem to stop people."

He shrugged. "I don't like it when people try to get me to do things, so I try to make it a habit not to get people to do things if they really don't want to. Ultimately, they're the ones who have to live in their own lives, and they know what makes sense for themselves more than anyone else could. Plus, there's no way in a million years I could ever make you do anything you don't want to do."

"That's true," Ellie said. "I'm very stubborn."

He laughed. Up ahead, he could see the farm.

They walked right up the main road until they were there at the front gates, where two people stood guard by a big metal barrel that had a fire going in it. They both had shotguns.

"Hey, Ellie. Who's this?" one of them, a tanned human guy probably David's age, asked. His silent partner was a jag guy with orange fur who was really thin and wiry.

"A friend of mine. He helped me take down the giant," Ellie replied.

"Don't suppose you have any proof of that?"

"Well, you can go take a walk and find the corpse. It isn't exactly hard to find."

"I believe her," the other man said.

The first stared at her, then shrugged. "Okay. Thanks. Wait right here."

He walked over to a small wooden hut nearby and disappeared into it, then returned a few seconds later holding a cloth sack. He passed it to Ellie, who took it and began digging through it. "Here, open your pack, David."

"Okay," he replied, crouching down beside her, shrugging out of his pack and unzipping it. She passed him three ears of corn, four cans marked 'mixed vegetables', four potatoes, and several nice cuts of beef wrapped in wax paper and tied with twine.

"Looks good. I'll be back around in a few days to see if anything needs doing," Ellie said as she transferred the rest to her own pack. "And if you see him come around looking for work, you should consider hiring him. He's good and I vouch for him. His name is David."

"All right, I'll relay that to the boss," the first man said.

They finished packing up and left, beginning to walk back in the direction of David's homestead. "Thank you for that," he said.

"Not a problem. You did good out there." After another few minutes of walking, she stopped and turned to face him as he stopped with her. "Well, this is where we part ways, I'm afraid. I have things to do and people to see. I'll swing by in two or three days and see if there's anything I could help with," she said.

"Okay. Um, thank you. I really appreciate that."

"Well, you three are good people. And there aren't enough of those in the world, and I like having good people in my life if I can manage it," she said.

She gave him a hug and a lingering kiss on the mouth, then smirked at him as she pulled back slightly, probably happy with the result she'd produced. Then she turned around and walked away. David found his eyes drawn to her extremely toned, shapely ass. He was *really* looking forward to seeing her again.

He resumed his walk home.

...

They ate well that night, frying up the beef and preparing the ears of corn.

David made a soup of potatoes and vegetables, and all three of them sat together in the basement and shared stories and laughed. They ate, and then sat around, letting the food settle.

"When do you think we should start moving?" April asked.

"Within the next few days," David replied. "Probably shouldn't wait too long. It's a pretty prime spot, and right now we're the ones who control it...sort of. I guess, we're the ones who know of it and are apparently going to live there. We should act before that changes."

"I agree," Evelyn said. She looked at David intently. "So...you should expand more on what you did with Ellie."

"Uh, I mean, we did several things," he replied, laughing a little awkwardly.

"Oh don't bullshit me, David. Come on, I want details of you banging that pussy of hers," Evelyn said, leaning closer.

"I have to admit, I do too. Ellie is *very* attractive. I would *love* to have sex with her," April murmured.

"All right, all right, so she dragged me to this cabin..."

By the time he was done filling them in, they were both staring at him intently, and both looked like they were ready to be filled in in a different way.

"Can we have a threesome?" he asked after several seconds of silence passed following his wrap-up of the story.

"Yes!" both Evelyn and April replied at once.

"Okay, awesome. Let's do this."

All three of them got up and hurriedly went through the prep for amazing sex, stripping and washing and gathering in the bed. David watched as Evelyn and April began to make out. April seemed a little tentative, as if unsure if Evelyn would be happy with the advances, but Evelyn immediately began to return the kissing with a passionate zeal.

April looked very pleasantly surprised. It was really fucking hot to watch. David moved forward until he was in the right place and began licking one of Evelyn's amazingly sexy pink nipples. She moaned into the kiss and he felt her shudder as he begin to pleasure her.

Soon, he was sucking on one of her enormous breasts. He loved feeling all her naked skin against his, rubbing together, feeling her body shift and twitch as pleasure sparked through her like electric shocks. After a bit, he saw April join him, sucking on her other breast. They locked eyes and he saw a lot of happiness there, and a lot of desperate sexual need. He intended to satisfy that need. For tonight, at least.

It was sure to be back soon.

He shifted up, now kissing Evelyn, locking lips with hers, tasting her, feeling her tongue twining with his in eager lust. He loved the way she interrupted their kissing unintentionally whenever the pleasure of what April was doing to her was too much. Especially now that April had moved on to her pussy and was rubbing her clit now.

"Oh April, yes!" she cried as she hit a particularly sensitive spot.

"Do you want me to eat you out, Evelyn?" April asked.

"Oh fuck yes, *please* do that," she replied immediately.

"While she's doing that, there's something I have been dying to do with you," David said as he sat up.

"What? Whatever it is, I'm pretty sure I'll let you do it," Evelyn replied.

"I want to tit-fuck you."

"Oh. Well, that makes sense. Yeah, do it. Then you can put it in my mouth."

He quickly climbed on top of her and settled his cock between her enormous breasts, then he grasped them, shuddering at touching them because of how just fucking erotic it was. They were *so big*. He was still having a hard time processing that. He pressed them together and started doing it, sliding his cock back and forth between her tits.

It didn't feel as good as fucking her pussy or her mouth, but it was still a fantastic experience. Evelyn had this perfect combination of having breasts that were so large that they were almost gratuitous, and yet they weren't, because on her over seven-foot frame, they looked pretty natural.

David kept it up, slipping his cock back and forth between them, staring into her eyes as he did that, and then finally wanted to put it in her mouth really bad. Actually, he wanted to fuck her mouth. He moved forward and slipped his cock right into her mouth.

"I'm gonna fuck your mouth, okay?" he asked.

"Mmm-hmm," she agreed, closing her lips firmly around his shaft.

He groaned as he felt her start sucking, then he grabbed her big head and began thrusting, pushing his cock as far as it would go into her mouth.

He loved her big mouth and all the things she could do with it, all the things she was willing to do with her tongue and her lips...and her throat. He grunted as he shoved his dick really deep into her mouth, hit the back of her throat and went a little down it, and kept it there.

"Swallow," he said, then groaned loudly as she did. "Fuck...again, babe."

She swallowed again, and several more times, and at some point he couldn't help it, he started letting off down her throat.

"Oh fuck! Oh Evie!" he moaned as he held her head and kept his cock partway down her throat, coming hard.

She let him stay there like that, still swallowing

over and over again, clenching all those wet, hot muscles around the head of his orgasming dick, accepting all of his seed. He moaned loudly, grunting occasionally, totally locked into place by his rapture, lost in the ecstasy as he emptied his seed into her mouth.

She sucked everything he had to give and swallowed it all.

When he was done, he pulled out of her mouth and sat down beside her. She moaned and shifted, and he realized April was still at work.

"Thank you so much, babe," he said. "That was just amazing."

"You're–oh! Yes!–welcome, dear. I'm glad you enjoy it so much."

"I thoroughly did," he said, grabbing the lube and rubbing his cock down. "And now I'm going to go enjoy April's vagina."

She mumbled something affirmative and kept on eating Evelyn out. She seemed really into it. Once he was lubed up, he got behind her. She was laying flat on her stomach, which worked fine for him. The only minor problem was her tail, so he couldn't lay flat against her, but whatever, he could work around that.

He looked down at her tight, fit ass and her slim thighs and her sexy, sexy tail, which was shifting back and forth. Resting the head of his dick at the slick, light-green entrance of her pussy, he began working his way into her.

"Mmm!" April moaned, muffled, as he got inside of her.

"You are *very* tight, April," he said to her as he continued inching his way into her.

She raised her head briefly. "It's because you're so fucking big, David," she replied, then moaned loudly as he finished getting inside of her.

"Ready to get fucked hard?" he asked.

"Yes, I really, *really* am," she moaned, and resumed eating Evelyn out.

He started fucking her, slowly ramping up, building the speed and strength of his thrusting, shoving himself again and again into her pussy. She did feel incredibly fucking tight tonight and the pleasure was burning through him. He definitely wasn't done yet, he had probably another two orgasms to blow off.

He looked down at his cock sliding in and out of her crazy tight rep pussy, and loved the way it looked and felt, especially with him really fucking giving it to her. She was screaming now, her voice muffled as she continued furiously eating out Evelyn, who'd had at least one orgasm by now, and looked like she was on her way to two.

April looked so good with her face buried in Evelyn's crotch, and the little up-and-down motions her head made were very subtle, but he *loved* seeing them because it really helped accentuate the fact that she was doing that because she was licking at Evelyn's clit over and over again. And Evelyn's huge pale thighs, fuck!

They were amazing, especially with her legs spread wide and her hands on her knees, looking like some kind of sex deity, this enormous goddess of sex and love and pleasure, her huge, immense tits shifting and jiggling.

He reached down, holding himself up with one arm, and wrapped his fingers around April's tail. He felt her tense, then he began to massage it, running his fingers up and down it. She shuddered violently and let out a very loud, intense moan of pleasure.

He made her come within about twenty seconds.

"Oh fuck, April, *yes...*" he groaned loudly as her vagina clenched and spasmed around his cock, upping the pleasure intensely. He kept screwing her until she was finished, and then pulled out of her. Evelyn had another orgasm, her whole body spasming, her huge boobs jiggling amazingly as she came. When she was finished, he patted April's ass.

"Move aside, April, I want Evelyn's pussy now."

"You got it," she replied sedately, and moved out of the way.

As soon as he was able, he climbed on top of Evelyn, slipped his cock into her ridiculously wet pussy, and began fucking her. She moaned loudly and he joined her. Her pussy felt incredibly good right now, an intense burst of absolute pleasure.

"Oh, Evie..." he moaned loudly.

"Yes, David, fuck me honey," she replied. "Fuck me so good..."

He kept screwing her, pounding her, for several minutes. And then, he felt an intense urge to switch positions.

"Let's do doggystyle," he said, pulling out of her.

"You got it," she replied, flipping over and getting onto her hands and knees, showing him her enormous pale ass. "April, you want me to return the favor?"

"Oh yes, that would be amazing, thank you," April replied, taking up Evelyn's previous position quickly. Once she was settled into place, Evelyn lowered her big head and began to lick April's clit, making their slim rep friend moan loudly in beautiful pleasure. David quickly got up against Evelyn and slipped back inside of her.

"Oh fuck, Evelyn, this is so awesome. Your ass

is so huge!" he groaned, and slapped her enormous, thick, pale ass. She moaned and he did it again, harder, leaving a red handprint. That was so fucking satisfying. He kept slamming into her from behind, really giving it to her, pounding the absolute fuck out of her goliath pussy, and this time he couldn't keep from coming. His orgasm was bursting out of him and there was no stopping it.

"*EVIE, FUCK! YES!*" he screamed as he started coming inside of her.

It felt like a seismic event, like his whole body was being shaken by the tremendous enormity of its power. It was like a supernova going off in his core. Waves, intensely powerful waves of absolute, unbridled pleasure shot out and its power surprised him.

Apparently he *really* liked doing it doggystyle with Evelyn. His whole body contracted as he thrust his cock forward, shoving it as deep and as hard as he could in automatic reaction to the arrival of the orgasm, and the first thick volley of his seed sprayed out of him and began hosing down her insides.

He pumped her vagina full of his seed in hard spurts, each one sending a fresh explosion of passionate ecstasy throughout the whole of his being. He could hear himself moaning and grunting and crying out, feel his hands on Evelyn's enormously broad hips, feel his own hips thrusting forward in time with his orgasm.

Everything else was the blinding bliss of the climax.

At some point, eventually, he finished. And when he did, he immediately pulled out of her and fell onto his side, gasping for breath, his vision whiting out.

"Holy shit, I thought that was going to kill you,"

he heard April say.

"Yeah babe, goddamn, what was *that* about? I knew my pussy was good, but *wow.*"

"Dunno. But it felt fucking awesome. I think I just *really* like doing you doggystyle, and also watching you go down on April. Plus, I just really like both of you."

"I like you too, David," Evelyn said with a grin.

"Yeah, same," April murmured. She yawned. "I'm tired."

David nodded weakly. "Same. I think we need to sleep."

"I'll tend to everything for the night, you two sleep. I'll be to bed soon," Evelyn said.

"Thank you, Evie," David said as he got beneath the blankets.

"Yeah, thanks Evelyn, you're the best," April said, yawning again and getting in next to him. He wrapped an arm around her and held him close, and she pressed herself against him. "Thank you. I feel safe like this," she whispered.

"I'm glad, April," he said, and kissed her forehead.

Within a minute, he was out like a light.

...

David opened his eyes and laid frozen in his bed.

He'd heard something–

A thump overhead. Evelyn shifted beside him. "What was that?" she whispered, staring at him in the reddish gloom of the fire they had left going for heat. It was almost dead now.

"I don't know," David whispered.

They froze as they heard a voice overhead, then

another. April came awake. "What is it?" she whispered, sounding terrified.

"People," David said as he threw the blanket aside and got up. He snatched his pistol from off the table where he'd left it and then pulled on some boxers and his pants. There were definitely people upstairs.

Before he could say anything else or try to devise a plan of how to deal with it, he heard the door rattle as someone tried to open it.

"April, get over into the nook there, to the left of the stairs. Hide there," he whispered harshly.

"Okay," she said, and got up, holding a blanket around her. She hurried over and disappeared into the gloom there.

"Evelyn, over there," he whispered, pointing to the right.

She nodded and got up against the wall, her pistol in hand. The fact that she was naked did nothing to lessen how intimidating she looked. He shifted so that he wasn't directly in line of sight, but could still get a clear view of the stairwell.

Suddenly, the door at the top of the stairs was kicked open. He heard footsteps, slow ones, moving down the first short flight of stairs, then coming onto the landing, then moving around...

"I think someone's down here–fuck!" A lone figure appeared at the landing and froze.

"Get. Out. Now," David said slowly and firmly, his pistol raised, covering the man.

"What the fuck...you're the asshole who was at the fucking village!" He began raising his pistol.

David was already aiming, so he squeezed the trigger. The shot nailed the bastard in the face. He fell and immediately David began to hear shouting, and people coming. He cursed and readied himself, he heard running footsteps, but this time the person stopped before coming into view.

"You fucking bastards! You killed him!" the person snapped.

"I warned him to get out. I'm giving you the same warning. Get the *fuck* out of my house and I won't have to kill you," David replied.

"Oh fuck you, you fucking–"

This time, Evelyn fired.

Apparently she had a shot on him and put it to use. He heard a few other people shout. He waited. There was what sounded to be a heated debate between two or three people, their voices a bit more audible now that the door to the upstairs was open and they must be speaking nearby. He prepared himself for a more brutal assault, unsure about their odds, especially if they had something to toss down here, like a grenade or something on fire.

But abruptly they heard retreating footfalls.

Several seconds of silence passed as the footfalls ceased. Five seconds became ten, ten became thirty.

"Are they gone?" Evelyn whispered finally.

"I think so. Wait here," David replied, and began to make his way forward.

He got to the stairs and waited, listening. Still nothing. He began moving up them and double-checked the two bodies. They were definitely dead. He moved carefully around into the upper stairwell and looked through the partially open door. He couldn't see much, but there was enough moonlight coming in that he could at least see a little.

There didn't appear to be any people.

He kept going and soon slipped into the main room.

The front door was open, and he spied retreating bootprints in the snow, leading away from the cabin, mixing with several leading towards it. So, someone had showed up, attempted to rob them, and then bailed when it got too difficult. Well, this fucking sucked. Although it had netted them a few more guns and whatever supplies the two dicks who they'd shot had on them.

David checked the exterior, then came back inside and closed the doors as best he could.

"We're okay," he said as he came back down. "You can come out now, April. They're gone."

"Fuck, that was so fucking scary," she whispered as she came out from her hiding place. He held out an arm to her and she immediately came over and pressed against him. He wrapped his arm around her, holding her.

"Yeah," he muttered. "That fucking sucked."

"Now what?" Evelyn asked as she approached.

He looked at April, then he looked up at her. "We're not waiting to leave any longer. We're going to start moving tomorrow at dawn."

# ABOUT ME

I am Misty Vixen (not my real name obviously), and I imagine that if you're reading this, you want to know a bit more about me.

In the beginning (late 2014), I was an erotica author. I wrote about sex, specifically about human men banging hot inhuman women. Monster girls, alien ladies, paranormal babes. It was a lot of fun, but as the years went on, I realized that I was actually striving to be a harem author. This didn't truly occur to me until late 2019-early 2020. Once the realization fully hit, I began doing research on what it meant to be a harem author. I'm kind of a slow learner, so it's taken me a bit to figure it all out.

That being said, I'm now a harem author!

Just about everything I write nowadays is harem fiction: one man in loving, romantic, highly sexual relationships with several women.

I'd say beyond writing harems, I tend to have themes that I always explore in my fiction, and they encompass things like trust, communication, respect, honesty, dealing with emotional problems in a mature way…basically I like writing about functional and healthy relationships. Not every relationship is perfect, but I don't really do drama unless the story actually calls for it. In total honesty, I hate drama. I hate people lying to each other and I hate needless rom-com bullshit plots that could have been solved by two characters have a goddamned two minute conversation.

Check out my website
www.mistyvixen.com

Here, you can find some free fiction, a monthly newsletter, alternate versions of my cover art where the ladies are naked, and more!

Check out my twitter
www.twitter.com/Misty_Vixen

I update fairly regularly and I respond to pretty much everyone, so feel free to say something!

Finally, if you want to talk to me directly, you can send me an e-mail at my address:
mistyvixen@outlook.com

Thank you for reading my work! I hope you enjoyed reading it as much as I enjoyed writing it!

-Misty

51639085R00132